The Night of the Past

Margaret Gregory

Also by Margaret Gregory

TYMOREAN TRUST SERIES
THE THIRD GENERATION SERIES
ATAPI SORCERESS SERIES
MAEVEN DRAGON THIEF SERIES
TOUCHING OTHER LIVES SERIES

when things were sorted out, but the police let the boyfriend go. I went to talk to him, to tell him Elena was married to Marcus, and to suggest he let them alone."

"What happened when you spoke to him?"

"I got no answer by phone, and no one was at his place. I had the owner of the cabin go to check it and he found no one there. But if they had a baby being looked after somewhere, maybe they went there and the ex-boyfriend found them. The guy disappeared about then, right off the grid. Suspicious if you ask me."

Kim did a semblance of her former self.

After a while, Bray said, "I am sorry I didn't have better news."

"No...it's okay...I just wanted to understand."

"I could ask the police if they have learnt anything else in the last decade," Bray offered. "If you could give be your contact details."

Kim debated about that, and just gave an email address and her mobile phone number.

"Do you have a residential address?"

"No, I am staying with friends just now. Next week I will be heading interstate to visit other friends."

"No worries, then. I will see what I can do."

"Thank you, Mr Bray."

Chapter 22: Bray Causes Trouble

Kim kept to her persona all the way down in the lift and while crossing the ground floor lobby. Outside, she went to the nearest tram stop and caught the first tram that came along. She only went one stop and from there walked to the café where she was to meet Grant and Paula. Adam arrived a short while later.

"No one seemed interested in her," Adam confirmed.

"Is that what kept you?" Kim asked. Her voice quavered a bit, in relief from being away from Bray. "I can't see that snake racing out to see where I go, nor any other of the yuppies that work there."

"So what did he have to say," Grant asked.

"That Marcus was like a son to him and to his knowledge had no children. He implied Marcus and Elena married in a hurry because Elena was already pregnant from someone else. He mentioned a very long honeymoon and when Marcus returned he would have changed his will if he then had a child. He tried to imply I was Eugene Bennett's bastard," Kim told them. "He's smooth, to have come up with all that just then."

"A lot of it is the truth," Grant pointed out. "A lot of it fits with what we know."

"Yes, but his time line is out," Kim pointed out. "Especially as I fudged my age upward by two years."

"Was there more?" Adam prompted.

"He kept the copy of the birth certificate, and the title, and promised to look into things. But before that he was hell bent on blaming Bennett for the disappearance. Claimed he went to warn Marcus, but they had gone and some thug was on the floor. He said later, Marcus had called him in a panic, needing a place to go, and he gave them the address of a cabin he used at times." Kim went on to mention the rest of the conversation.

They ordered eats and drinks. Kim was glad to have something else to think on, as her knee and Adam's touched lightly.

"That bit about the will is interesting," Grant decided. "I think it means Bray knew where Marcus's will was. Which could be if he had helped Marcus write it. Yet, I agree on something. I am sure Marcus would have changed his will once you came along, Kim.

Chapter 21: Confronting Bray

The desire to confront Bray grew in intensity. Kim hated putting it off, but she didn't want to do it alone. Both Adam and Grant had end of the year exams as did she. It had to wait.

The wait did give her time to think through various scenarios and try to come up with reasons to visit him, without spooking him. Bray had an office in Twin Falls, where he had a small law practice. He also had an office in the city, as he was a member of a prestigious law firm that dealt with wills, business law and civil suits.

After the last exams, Gavin invited Paula, Kim and Adam out to tea at a family style restaurant to celebrate finishing. Adam was happy to go, even though his school friends had plans to party down at the beach. He had a deeper desire that was starting to drive him crazy. Kim had made a bargain with him, a promise, to keep her feelings secret until she was eighteen. Part of that was proving to the world who she really was. At that time, she hoped her mother would explain to her step-father the truth. Yet, to be safe, she wanted to find out how her birth parents had died, and where they were.

Bray was the link to all of it. She was sure.

The restaurant was not near where they lived and busy enough that the ambient noise masked their strategy session.

"Why the city office," Paula asked.

"Because his office in Twin Falls isn't mentioned on his profile at Bell Masson and Willand or on his social media pages. He spends most of his time in the city," Grant explained.

"Will they even let her make an appointment?" Paula persisted.

"I think, if certain concepts are mentioned," Grant began.

"Grant...." Paula mock threatened.

"Okay, Bray, as we now know, was a witness at the wedding of Kathryn's parents. He is probably one of very few people who know they were actually married. I bet he does not know about Kathy. We also know he was the one to have her parents declared dead. He approached your Aunt Grace while 'settling the estate'.

From what my friend can find out, both Marcus and Elena were only children, and he can't trace any close relatives. Bray is, however, a second cousin once removed of Elena.

"Bray produced a will that he presented for probate. Pretty standard, leaving all to his wife. And if they both died together, money to go to some specific charities, coincidentally managed by Duncan Bray."

"The skunk," Paula summarised. "The problem is, and I think Kim had better make a will of her own, that Marcus's estate still isn't fully settled."

"Really?" Adam interjected. "After 13 years? How come?"

"It seems there is a large cash sum that is still unaccounted for," Grant revealed. He had a faint grin on his face, but didn't explain further.

"So...what assets did get settled?" Paula asked. She glanced at Kim, who was surely the rightful beneficiary.

"Property investments," Grant said, shrugging.

"So what happens if a proper heir turns up now?" Adam asked.

"Bray gets rattled," Grant warned. "So that is why I suggest when Kim goes to see him, she doesn't let on she knows what her parents were worth. In fact, seeming like her old self, young and naïve, will be the least threatening move."

"I can do that," Kim told her friends. "If there is one thing I now appreciate about his freak memory I have, is no one except you three really know about it. I can let him waffle on and pick up on discrepancies."

"Okay, we will discuss suitable questions to ask once we have an appointment," Grant decided. "Any questions?"

"It sounds pretty certain that Bray wanted Marcus's fortune," Kim said. "But have you considered, if he is a cousin to Elena's mother, he could have a claim on the estate through that? Definitely to Elena's mother's residual fortune."

"I hadn't forgotten," Grant assured her. "I still don't know how to approach seeing her. But if Bray admits you could be Elena's child, which could be a reason."

"No, he doesn't know of me. He will likely think I am pulling a con," Kim decided.

"Let's see what happens when you met him," grant suggested.

Table of Contents

Chapter 1: Getting Away

"What's wrong, pal?" Grant asked. He'd seen me wince from the friendly shoulder thump.

"Nothing," I lied. The cause was the beating my very correct step-father had given me the night before. That and the overwhelming sense of humiliation from the sermon that followed.

"You still want to go hiking?"

"Yes."

Grant had two packs almost ready. I'd only had to add a change of clothes and a toiletries bag.

"Where are we going?" I asked. We were in Grant's home territory, a good twenty miles from where I lived with my mum, sister and step-father.

"Golden Falls," Grant told me.

I echoed the name. I'd heard of the place, but couldn't recall who mentioned it.

"So, what's the mystery about that place?"

Grant's passion was trying to solve real life mysteries, not that he'd had any success so far.

"A supposedly haunted house. The owners mysteriously disappeared on their way home from a dance, about fifteen years ago."

"So, where is Golden Falls?"

"About half an hour's drive north of here."

"How did you hear of it? Or have you known about it for a while?"

I had assumed Grant had already checked out all the local places.

"No, actually. I only just heard about the place. Paula mentioned it."

A painful prickle erupted all over my still very sore back. I recalled then, being asked by my sister, Kim, "Where is Golden Falls."

Even thinking so fleetingly of Kim, caused heat to flush my face. I turned quickly to heft one of the packs, and concentrate on not wincing. Obviously, I failed.

"I have a supply of painkillers if a dose would help," Grant offered.

"Hell, yes," I admitted. Grant was my very best friend. "How did you know?"

"Your sister said something to Paula, but all I got told was that Kim was practically hysterical. What did you do to upset the old goat this time?"

"Drop it will you, Grant? It was nothing. Kim and I were just mucking around, like we've always done since we were kids. Mock fighting, arguing about nothing."

"Aren't you two a bit too old for that now?" Grant sighed. "Does he know where you are?"

"No, but he told me to keep out of his sight."

"Is Kim alright?"

"He doesn't believe in hitting girls." Of that I was sure, but he had probably given her as bad a sermon as the one he'd given me – full of threats of hell and brimstone. And what they did in bible times to women who...my mind sought for a polite euphemism... had loose morals. We hadn't been doing anything.

Grant went on talking, guessing I didn't want to say anymore. "Well, Kim went over to Paula's and she said they were going to do some retail therapy."

Paula, Grant's girlfriend, was also, Kim's best friend and had been since they were both little. Paula had always accepted Kim's... oddness...when others had laughed at her for being slow, or retarded. I knew she was neither. At home, when she felt safe, she was very quick minded and learnt quickly. At school, though, she couldn't seem to communicate what was in her mind to others. She'd stammer, or seem to forget what she was trying to say. Her early teachers had not tried to help her but the special teachers she'd had in recent years had discovered that if allowed the time to answer questions, verbally or in writing, with no pressure, she could answer with a high degree of accuracy.

"Do you need to call your mother?" Grant prompted.

"No. I sent her a text message." That was an old secret I had shared with him. It was an even older game that my mother had begun after Kim had come to live with us – long before she had remarried.

"We had been kids, and no doubt she had not wanted to frighten us. The game was her way of getting us to assess how safe we felt.

If we met someone who gave us a bad feeling, we were to tell her. It was, looking back, a kind of code.

The message I had sent was that I was okay, not that I was angry, sore and confused, even though I was. It meant that I understood why I'd been punished. My step-father had taken what he'd seen, totally misunderstood, and acted according to his strict churchy ways.

Grant broke my reverie. "Well, let's get going. I thought we'd drive to Twin Falls, that's the nearest town, and park the car there. We can hike along the tourist trails from there."

"Great, I can use the fresh air." I meant that as meaning, 'being away from my step-father'.

"Did Paula say where they were going?"

"No, the pair of them were being mysterious."

It was probably a good thing I'd be away from Kim for a while. I needed to sort out some very odd feelings.

Chapter 2: Sneaking About

"What will your step-father say if he sees you in jeans?" Paula asked. Kim had just come back from the ladies change room to swap her clothes for the new jeans and brushed cotton shirt.

"He won't say anything if I don't wear this at home, at church or when I am not hiking."

Paula wasn't so sure, but she kept quiet.

As if Kim sensed that, she went on, "We have to have a track suit for sport at school. He didn't object to that. And this shirt is modest enough, not like what Brittany and Hazel like to wear."

"True, I guess. Are you sure you want to do this hike?"

"Yes. I'm tired of being left out of things. I know I can keep up with you."

"Well, we need to hurry if we want to catch the bus to Twin Falls in time to meet the boys."

On the bus, around strangers, Paula did the chattering and Kim just nodded and watched out the window. She wondered, as she often did, what caused Kim to be scared most of the time. She could understand loud people being frightening, and the boys in class being boisterous. At school, most teachers didn't tolerate slowness. She kept her sigh totally internal. Kim was her friend, she didn't have a mean bone in her body. At home, she could be quite animated, some of the time. The rest...Paula privately blamed Kim's step-father. When she'd been old enough to consider the idea, she wondered why Adam's mum had married him.

Kim hadn't said exactly why her step-father had been angry with her and Adam. She had just been so upset, by him punishing Adam. Paula compared the reaction to what her own parents would have done – grounded her – if she had made them really mad. Though Kim's step-father hadn't stopped her from going to stay with a friend for the weekend. Nor had he stopped Adam going off with Grant.

An idea occurred to her, as to why Kim wanted to join the boys for the hike. Her step father wouldn't know she was joining her brother.

"Do you think this is a good idea?" Paula asked her silent friend, not expecting an answer.

"I want to see Golden Falls," came the quiet answer.

"What's there?"

"I don't know."

It was the same answer se had got when Kim had first asked where the place was.

Paula sighed again. She knew the preparations Grant had made, including having two lightweight tents that could each sleep two. She had suggested to Kim to get a small hiking pack to carry her change of clothes and necessities. She wondered if Kim had even thought about such things.

Actually, she wondered what Kim's parents would say if they knew they were going hiking – with or without the boys. Her own folks were okay, since she would have Kim with her. Adam's mum would probably feel the same, except she usually chose to accept her husband's edicts.

"This is Twin Falls," Paula told Kim, and was relieved when her friend became more animated. She was quiet again while they waited for their packs to be unloaded from the storage bay. Paula had to point them out.

"Come on. Grant said to meet them at your aunt's place."

Grace Westcott had a huge smile when she saw Kim and Paula at the door. Kim threw herself at her aunt before even taking off her pack.

"I wish you would visit more often," Kim told her aunt.

"I know it would be nice, but I have a busy life here."

"Where are Grant and Adam," Paula asked.

"Gone to get some food for your hike. We can have a cuppa while we wait."

"Yes, please," Kim agreed. Paula wordlessly helped take her pack off, before removing her own.

"How have you been, Kim dear?"

Not a word of the previous day's drama was mentioned, just a babble of school trivia. Paula wondered if she had forgotten.

Paula explained, "They have some new support teachers. One of them is really helping."

"That is good to hear. My sister said you are getting better marks, Kim."

Kim didn't answer, just followed her aunt into the kitchen to help make the promised drink.

"So where are you headed?" Grace asked.

"Golden Falls," Kim told her. Paula noticed a change on Aunt Grace's expression before she answered.

"The falls are not the same since they built the dam up river from there."

"What else is around here?" Paula asked.

"Not a lot. It's just a really nice natural area. Hikers and fishermen come up here."

Sounds at the back door heralded the return of the boys with the supplies for the trip. Kim's eyes went straight to Adam, who simply stared back as his face flushed.

"Fancy seeing you here," Grant said, grinning. "You had no trouble?"

"No, the trip was fine," Paula assured him.

Adam finally managed to say, "Hi, Sis. Ready to hike, I see."

"I didn't want to miss out," Kim told him.

Paula glanced at Grant, who shrugged slightly. Maybe, she decided, both Adam and Kim were feeling uncomfortable about whatever their step-father had lectured them about.

Chapter 3: TheAbandoned House

The falls had been a disappointment. Yes, water was coming down the rock face but it was barely enough to feed the creek when once it had fed a wide river. They didn't bother to climb to the top. Instead they travelled along the dried part of the old riverbed. Kim seemed to be in a trance, though she had no trouble keeping up. Adam had to grab her pack when Grant called a halt.

"If we are going to camp out tonight, we need to find a good site."

"Why not along the river?" Kim asked.

Grant glanced at the trickle and rolled his eyes. "I thought to head back up towards the road," he went on. "I like the idea of being near water, but the trickle coming down is hardly enough to keep the water moving. There will be a lot of mozzies here."

Kim looked mutinous until Grant checked his map and said, "There is a track up ahead that should lead to a deserted old house."

Paula saw Kim's instant interest.

"It's a bit of a mystery," Grant continued. "No one lives there now, or comes near it. We can camp near it and if one of the scattered showers they are predicting comes during the night, we can duck inside for shelter. All in favour?"

Adam nodded, he already knew Grant planned to go there, and Paula, seeing Kim was interested, nodded as well.

After another hour of walking, they stepped from native bush into an unexpectedly open area. Ahead of them, a once tall and proud two storey house looked old, crumbling – its spirit broken. Saplings had sprung up in a few places close to the house, and grass grew between the pavers on a wide patio.

"People say this place is haunted," Gavin claimed.

"Are you sure we should be here?" Paula asked. She examined the cracked façade where sections of the texted paint had fallen away, revealing native rock. She also eyed how close the vegetation had grown to the house. In places, boughs nearly touched the roof.

"I researched the house," Grant assured her. "Depending on who you talk to, the place is either haunted by the young couple who lived here, or it's a place to avoid if you don't want to disappear."

"I don't," Paula told him.

"Afraid of ghosts?" Adam suggested instead.

"No. I don't believe in them. Do you really think you can figure out what happened to the couple?"

"Of course. I'm Grant Fletcher, mystery solver."

"So, why is the house still empty," Adam challenged him.

"It belonged to the couple, and even though they have been declared dead, they are not able to find any relatives. Supposedly they have advertised all over the state, possibly all over the country, for relatives to come forward. I think, if no one does by the end of this year, the place will be seized by the council and the property either sold or added to the state park."

"If they do that, we wouldn't be able to come here," Kim said, unexpectedly. "It would be sad." She began to walk over towards the door they could see, as if the house was calling to her. The others quickly followed.

"You aren't planning to go inside," Paula hinted to Kim. "It would be breaking and entering."

"The door might be open, and the house might like to have people in it again," Kim insisted.

"Kim, what say we find a place to put up the tents, then look around," Adam suggested.

Kim turned to Grant, waiting for him to decide where to have the tents. When he didn't, Kim wandered towards the side of the house, and stopped where the stones did.

"This is perfect," Grant exclaimed. He turned to consider the area. It has a little fence around it that we can sit on. The grass isn't that high, and we don't have to sleep on stones or try to hit pegs into stones. The house and the trees will protect us if the wind gets up. That's the way storms around here usually come from.

Kim had dropped her pack and gone to look at a wide old tree growing in what must have once been an ornamental garden. Paula noticed white roses blooming on overgrown rose bushes and went for a closer look.

"Hey," she said a bit later. "The front door is just around here."

Adam and Grant had dumped their packs and now come to see what she had discovered. Grant, took a photo of the closed front door, and the double row of rosebushes that encroached on a stone path that led away from the front door. Adam looked to see where Kim was and decided to pluck one of the roses that looked perfect even if the bush had not been tended. He took it with him to see what had Kim mesmerised.

"Hey, Kim. This is for you," Adam said, in a teasing tone.

When she turned, and smiled at the offering, he was relieved. Kim hadn't been herself at all since they began the hike. It felt like she was shunning him. A voice in his head said, "And she probably should."

He carefully put the rose on her palm, seeing a trace of red on an outer petal from when he had pricked his finger.

Chapter 4: Memories Returning

Kim stared at the unexpected gift, her heart suddenly beating faster than normal. Then she saw the tiny red blood drop. It was like a silent tear for having to squash how she truly felt for Adam. Tears welled in her eyes and she looked down. Then she was no longer seeing the rose...

The rose bushes were carefully pruned and shaped, they were in two neat rows, bracketing the path from the front door to the road. A beautiful woman in a fashionable pink gown, her honey coloured hair braided in an intricate design, her creamy pale face flushing red on the cheeks. A man dressed in a tailored suit of a light tan emerged from the oak door at the front of the white walled house. He stopped by one of the rose bushes, plucked a white rose and moved to give the woman the gift. On the rose was a tiny drop of blood. It seemed to be a sign of a deep secret between the two. The man looked at her with tenderness as he took her arm and led her down the path.

Kim didn't want the vision to end. The couple had, what she deeply wished for, which she could never have with the one her heart cried out for. She wiped her shirt sleeve across her eyes.

"What's the matter? I thought you would like it," Adam said, uncomfortable with her reaction.

"I do," she whispered. "I was just thinking how nice this place would have been, back then, when people lived here."

Adam turned to see what she was looking at, saw close up the dirty textured paint, crumbling and falling away. The once varnished and polished wood door, mottled by weather and the spreading moss. He had to agree.

"Come on. We need to set up the tents."

Kim sighed, once again aware of the twitter of birds, the tang of eucalyptus, and the still warmth of the late afternoon. She turned and headed back to where Grant and Paula had gone. Adam followed, wondering what had set Kim off this time. He was glad this 'episode' hadn't lasted too long, or the others would worry about having let her come. They had not stayed long or they would have realised Kim had been so oblivious, she'd not heard him talking for a full five minutes. He wanted to hold her, like he did when she was younger and woke from a bad dream. This time, though, he had sensed something different. He couldn't describe the feeling. Then she turned and look right at him, and smiled. The spell was broken and he to force himself to relax and get his heart rate back to normal.

He almost walked into her when she stopped suddenly. She put a finger to her mouth and gestured around the corner. He understood when he glanced and saw Grant and Paula kissing. His gut felt like a goat had kicked it.

Being deliberately loud, he said, "Where do you think you want to pitch the tent we have for you and Paula?"

He stepped into the view of his friends a moment later, and noticed they had sprung apart.

Kim asked Paula for her idea for the tent location, as if she had not seen what she had. She deferred to Grant.

"I thought in that corner, near the tree. It looks solid enough that it won't drop branches on us if there is a wind."

"Girls on one side of it, us on the other," Adam clarified.

"Sounds good," Paula agreed. "What do we do first?"

"Well, Adam and I can do the tents. Why don't you and Kim find a pump or a tap for some water? Here..."

Grant rifled through his pack and produced a folded plastic water holder. He tossed it at Paula.

Paula had to nudge Kim, breaking her scrutiny of the tree. "Hey! We're the water detail.

"There's a pump at the back of the house," Kim said, out of the blue.

"Is there? I didn't see one. Come on and show me."

Oddly, Kim led her straight to it, across to the other side of the stone flagged terrace. It was hidden by a trellis and right next to an old gully trap.

"I kind of hoped for a tap, but I suppose, out here, they don't have piped water," Paula commented.

Kim laughed, "I guess not. This should work by pumping the handle."

"Yes, so let's try it. Open that water thing up, but don't put it under the spout yet."

Paula found the handle very stiff, and even though she tried with all her strength to move it, the handle didn't budge. "How about helping me," Paula asked pointedly.

Even two of them working together made no difference.

"There is a river down the bottom of the garden," Kim announced.

"What river? The one we were following earlier?"

"No. The river Parr." Kim frowned at Paula's confused stare.

"I doubt it's much bigger than the one we saw. All the creeks down this way dried up as a result of the dam."

"It's there, come and see," Kim insisted.

"Whoa!" Paula grabbed her friend. "Let's not just run off. I will see if the guys can get the pump working first. Then we won't have to lug a ton of water back here."

"Then can we go and look?"

"If we have enough light after setting up the camp." Paula hoped they hadn't.

Grant and Adam already had one tent up, and were sorting out the other when they returned.

"We found a pump, but can't get it to work," Paula announced.

The two boys left the tent and went to investigate. They managed to lift the lever, and force it down, but no water came out.

"You can try the river," Kim told them.

Paula supplied, "The River Parr."

Grant checked his map. "Well, I'll be...Okay, but it might be much like the one down from the falls. And if it is, probably the reason why the pump is useless. The river isn't full enough to fill the reservoir the pump gets the water from."

"Let's check it out," Adam suggested. "Better do it in daylight. How did you know about the river, Paula?"

"Kim mentioned it," she answered blandly. She saw both boys stop abruptly. "Why didn't you know about the river," she went on to needle Grant.

"I knew about it," he claimed. "I thought it went underground and didn't emerge until further downstream. It and the arm we followed, join up near Twin Falls. That's how the town got its name if you don't know."

With a mock flourish in Kim's direction, Grant said, "lead on, my lady."

They had approached the area from the side, Adam decided as Kim turned and walked down a slight slope, weaving between new growth trees, and barging through what once might have been a hedge. She seemed eager to see the river.

More trees grew beyond the old hedge. New growth like on the other side, was tall enough to hide any view of the river, until they abruptly walked out onto an area of high grass and the sound of rippling water. The pebbly river bed was wider than the one just down from Golden Falls.

"Not much of a river." Paula commented.

Adam saw the same intent stare come over Kim's face as she'd had near the house. Kim wasn't seeing the shrunken river.

"It's not just a river. It's our river," spoke a male voice, full of warmth.

Paula went on, "At least it's water.

Kim heard, *"Don't go near the water." Then a carefree laugh that came from herself.*

"What do you reckon, Grant? Is it drinkable?" Paula asked.

Grant squatted down next to the trickle and tasted some from his cupped palm. Adam and Paula watched as Kim wandered upstream, along the edge of the pebbles. Adam decided to follow her.

Footsteps padded softly along the grassy riverbank. They weren't her own. She heard the gentle trickle of the river, the water was crystal clear and wide. In the centre, a small rowing boat was drifting peacefully with the current. Kim watched from where she sat on a tartan rug. Someone nearby was humming a familiar tune.

In the boat were two people, the woman's face obscured by a blue parasol. Kim's mind told her, "Mama." The man had dark hair and was smiling that familiar loving smile. Their laughter floated across from the boat to the bank. "Papa." The lady lowered her sunshade, looked across to the bank and waved.

Shadows lengthened over the river and the boat began to return to the bank. Kim saw the bank coming closer, felt someone holding her back from the water. The lady had flowers and began tossing the blooms, one by one towards the bank. They fell short and began to drift downstream. Kim saw a small hand reach out to try to catch them, saw the glistening pebbles below the water.

The man and woman were still laughing as the boat reached the bank and the couple stepped from the boat. The hand holding her let go, and she was running to the man and woman. He swept her up, ruffled her hair and they both hugged her, then they began to walk.

They stopped at a tall eucalypt with mottled bark. The man's free hand brushed the trunk revealing a heart shaped blemish. Then the woman took her, and the man took something from his pocket, and did something to the tree.

Kim suddenly found herself staring at a tree. The people had gone, bushes had grown up around the tree. At first she looked higher up the tree to find the blemish. As she heard someone come up behind her, Adam she knew, she looked lower. A blemish caught her eye, just above her normal eye level. She reached out to knock a piece of loose bark from the tree, then another. Time had not obliterated what she knew was there – a heart shaped blemish. Only now, as her fingers traced the letters, she recognised them.

Adam had the same elusive feeling again except this time, Kim wasn't in a trance. In fact, her face when she looked at him, had a secretive, but satisfied smile, that changed to one that made his heart flutter. She traced the letters again, mouthing something he couldn't quite read.

"Here you are," Grant called out. "Thought you'd nicked off to avoid carrying the water."

"Kim found a clue for you, mystery solver," Adam said, pointing to the tree.

Chapter 5: Camping

"Brilliant, Watson," Grant crowed as he read the carved inscription. "Marcus loves, Elena Anok."

"Anok is an odd name," Paula commented. "Who do you think they were?"

"Marcus? Likely he's the guy who used to live here. Elena? His fiancée was Elena, but her family name was Kingsley. Maybe that's the K, but the rest?"

Kim traced the letters again, this time whispering, "Marcus loves Elena," then voicelessly repeated, "and K." Then she bestowed that knowing smile at Adam.

That, now he understood her meaning, sent shivers down his spine. The awakening of the residual pain distracted his mind from a vague formless hope.

"We'd best head back and finish setting up," Adam told the group. He wanted to ponder Kim's stranger than usual behaviour.

"And we look for wood on the way back," Grant directed.

In a surprising change of mood, "Kim challenged Paula to see who could collect the most kindling or small branches. Grant picked a larger dead branch and pointed Adam to another.

"Think this will do?" Grant asked.

"Are we intending to let the fire go all night?" Adam asked him.

"No, not in this heat. We can cover the embers if we want a fire in the morning."

The girls had hurried ahead, when Grant asked, "What's with Kim at the moment?"

"Darned if I know," Adam admitted, although that wasn't quite the truth.

They reached the campsite and found the wood stacked in a neat way, and the girls trying to erect the second tent. Grant found the small hatchet he carried in his hiking pack and began chopping the smaller branches. Adam took a small shovel for the pack he was using.

"I'm going to lift some stones from the terrace, if I can. Thought to use them to make a ring around the fire," Adam announced.

"Oh, right. I thought you were going to dig the hole for the loo."

"Might do that too," Adam agreed. It would help keep him away from the others for a while.

Adam returned to find the small fire blazing, with Paula and Kim overseeing something that smelt delicious. Grant was longing on a ground sheet, watching the girls at work. He patted the space beside him.

"Proper little homemakers, those two. Kim did a good job putting the rocks around the fire pit. How's the other pit?"

"Dug down about 40 cm. Left the little shovel in the dirt pile. The tarp I had just fit around it. It's tied to nearby trees. I was going to suggest running a guide rope from here to there. What do you think?"

"Actually, it's a great idea. We don't want to rush off in the dark and get lost."

Adam knew Grant was thinking of Kim, but it would be very dark here, so far from a town. Grant pushed himself up. Adrian groaned and did the same. "Let's do this before it's fully dark."

Full dark settled after a long twilight. The four campers, all tired after a long day, lay around the fire. Paula was close to Grant, and Adam and Kim shared a separate groundsheet, though with more distance between them, at least at first. Kim rolled over, coming closer to Adam, but immediately asked Grant, "Do you know any more about the house of the people?"

Kim wasn't looking at Adam, but he still had the idea her turning over was deliberately contrived. He felt his face heat up at the idea, and not from the fire. Had Kim developed feelings for him, other than sisterly affection? Had he encouraged her? Or as his step father insisted – had not discouraged her?

His step-father thought Kim was simple, and insisted it was up to him, Adam, to put an end to...? Heck, it wasn't like they'd kissed or something more. He always respected her privacy, and if she threw herself at him, there was always an overt reason. His thoughts swirled in circles. One of his teachers, back a year or so, had proposed that siblings emitted incompatible pheromones that usually caused disinterest in any kind of romantic notions, and those that fell in love had compatible ones.

Gavin nudged him with his foot. "You been asleep? I don't think you heard a word I said."

"Ah...no I didn't. It's been a long day."

"The girls have gone to use the loo and intend to call it a night."

Adam wasn't ready to sleep, so maybe he had dozed for a while. He told Grant he would stay up a while longer. His friend, instead of retreating to the tent, settled down beside him.

"So, what were you saying?" Adam asked him.

"There wasn't much. Marcus Ryman was heir to a fortune. Old family money, and he was already amassing more. Elena, his...well people believed they were going to get married, wasn't as rich, but she was also a sole heiress. Most theories as to why they disappeared claim the money was at the root of it. Other than that, pick an idea – someone will have already thought it."

"Did they have kids?" was Adam's next question.

"There's not even a hint anywhere online that they did."

"So, with them both gone, who inherited this house and their other assets?"

"That's where I find it gets interesting," Grant said thoughtfully. "Elena's father was still alive when she disappeared, so he left his money to his wife. His wife is now quite ill, but she keeps insisting Elena is still alive and will inherit everything of hers. No one knows exactly how her will is worded. The general idea is that since Elena and Marcus have been declared legally dead, she might leave her money to charity."

"And Marcus?"

"He didn't come from around here so no one has any theories."

"I suppose Marcus was the one who carved the heart on the tree," Adam mused.

"Probably," Grant decided.

They heard rustling and turned to see Kim crawling from the tent. She had not changed out of her day clothes and had a thin but warm hiking blanket around her.

Chapter 6: Thunderstorm Apparition

"Can't you sleep?" Grant asked.

"I'm cold and the ground is hard," Kim said.

Considering the night was still fairly warm, Adam hoped Kim wasn't coming down with something.

"Paula asleep?" Grant asked.

"Yes. I don't know how she can do it."

Adam tossed a couple more small pieces of branch on the fire that had started to die down. Kim inched closer to it as if needing the warmth. She pulled the blanket tighter around herself and sat on the groundsheet, hugging her knees and watching the fire. The light from the flames flickered on her face, and she seemed hypnotised by them.

The small stone ringed fireplace had been replaced by a blazing log fire in a sturdy stone hearth. Under her was a thick, warm carpet. It was chilly for a late November night and the fire had begun to warm the air, making her drowsy. Suddenly a loud clanging rent the air, waking her fully. About to let out a wail of fright, she was quickly picked up, her face pressing lightly into a soft wool cardigan. A voice hummed softly, reassuring her as she was carried up a winding staircase. Stern faces looked down from gilt frames. Familiar faces that didn't frighten her. A door opened in front of her, she was carried across to a small bed. The only light came in through the window from the full moon. In moments, she was in a warmed bed, and blankets were being tucked around her. Nearby, a soft voice sung familiar tunes. From downstairs, came loud voices.

The vision faded. Kim realised how stiff she was and moved to loosen up. Grant had finally turned in to sleep, so Adam and Kim were alone by the fire. When Kim moved, Adam framed a question.

"What is it about this place that gets to you?" His voice betrayed his anxiety. "You are moodier than I have ever known you to be."

Kim didn't answer for a while, then she said, "I don't know what it is. This place suggests things to me?"

"What sort of things?"

"People. Places. Things I don't remember seeing before. I can't have seen before, but yet they are so familiar."

"Why don't you turn in," Adam suggested.

"Can we go into the house tomorrow?"

"If it is locked up, we won't be breaking in."

"Maybe I will sleep by the fire," Kim suggested.

"You were cold before, and you have the sleeping bag in the tent. Go join Paula."

Obediently, like a child, Kim finally returned to the tent. Yet her behaviour was worrying Adam. He doubted he would sleep at all.

Thunder was rumbling in the distance as Kim followed the rope guide to the makeshift toilet. She had her torch with her, since she hated the dark. In recent times, she had learnt to hide such fears, but hey hadn't gone away. Using the folding seat, over a hole, was something she had never had to do and really didn't like. Still it was a better option than squatting somewhere in the dark. Once she had finished, and scooped dirt into the hole, she was more than ready to hurry back to the tent. Actually, she was pleased she had gone by herself. Having the rope to follow was reassuring. She was within sight of the tents when a blinding bolt of lightning lit up the area. Following instantly, came a massive crack of thunder. Her resolve to be an adult vanished. She screamed.

Adam heard the scream and rushed out of his tent, dragging a blanket with him. He saw the lit torch on the ground and ran for it. Kim was crouched on the ground, hands over her ears, shaking like a leaf in a strong wind. He helped her up, and put the blanket around her.

"It's okay, Kim. It was just thunder. I think we all jumped out of our skins."

Kim spotted a lantern coming from the house, she grabbed Adam and pointed.

"Hey! What's going on here?" a fierce voice yelled.

Adam spun around and felt Kim hiding behind him. He saw a face above the hurricane lamp – dark hair, dark beard, shadows making the face demonic. Kim gripped his arm, muttering, "You can't trust him. You can't trust him." She was shivering so hard, she felt it.

"Who are you?" the stranger demanded. "What are you doing here?"

Grant had emerged as soon as the stranger had yelled. Adam forced himself to be calm.

"Please, you don't need to shout. You are scaring my sister."

He stranger modulated his voice and repeated, "What are you doing here?"

Grant moved forward. "We stopped here to camp."

"This is private property," the man stated belligerently.

"Since when?" Grant asked. "As far as I was told, this place has been abandoned for years. I'm sorry if that isn't true. It was a safe spot, close to water. We'll be leaving in the morning."

The man backed down. "No. I should apologise. You couldn't have known. I only signed the paperwork today, and arrived late. When I heard the scream, it ...freaked me."

"I did get told this place was haunted," Grant remarked, as another bolt of lightning lit the sky. At least the thunder was further away.

Adam could still hear Kim murmuring, but he intended to remain calm. "My sister screamed. She has never been comfortable during thunderstorms. We didn't expect there to be one tonight, and it's a lot more immediate out here."

"It is. Look, I'm Eugene Bennett," the man introduced himself. "I'm pretty much camping inside myself tonight. You are more than welcome to move inside if you want to. Or if it rains. The latest forecast predicts there might be heavy falls."

"Thanks, but we are all set up out here," Adam told him.

"Then come up to the house in the morning. I will shout you breakfast. I brought a generator with me, so there will be power when I hook it up. I came to check the place over."

"We will see in the morning," Adam told him, not confirming the invitation. "If the storm doesn't move off, I doubt we'll sleep much until it does. We may sleep late."

"Any time then," Bennett accepted. "Oh, I should ask who my guests will be."

"Grant Fletcher, mystery solver."

Bennet laughed. "I begin to understand why you are here. I doubt you will figure out what the police couldn't."

Grant shrugged, and introduced the others by first names only.

Chapter 7: Recalling Bad Dreams

Kim stayed behind Adam until she was sure the stranger had really gone.

"Do you want to see inside the house?" Adam asked Kim.

Grant said, "I sure do."

Adam still felt Kim trembling. He wasn't sure if it was from the cold breeze that had sprung up, or because of the recent confrontation. "I reckon the guy is harmless."

"I'm sorry. The thunder scared me and this place is...well, the guy looked demonic."

"He sure did," Paula agreed. "Kim, let's get back in the tent. It's getting colder out here. We can put our foam mats close together and maybe share body heat if our sleeping bags are together."

"I don't think I can sleep with the storm around."

"You can put your radio on," Paula suggested.

"Yes. But I will put my earbuds in so it won't keep you awake," Kim offered.

The music kept the image of the dark haired man out of her head. And soon she relaxed enough to sleep. She switched off the radio and thought of an image that always made her feel safe. A bright room, with white walls decorated with yellow flowers. A window with stripes down it, bracketed by orange curtains. Around the room, toys on shelves, waiting to be played with.

Thunder rumbled in her dream, and she seemed to wake up, that familiar dream room around her, lit only by moonlight around her. The remnants of a bad dream still fresh in her mind. She didn't feel her feet move to the side of the bed and walk her to the door, but the door drew closer. It was slightly ajar, so she could open it, even though the door handle was out of her reach. There was shouting below, she followed the sound.

Halfway down the stairs, she stopped and peeped between the uprights of the bannister. Below was the bad man from her dream. She shoved her fist in her mouth, not wanting the bad man to see her. He was making her smiling mama look frightened.

"There you are, little one," the voice of her nanny said quietly. "You need to get back to bed."

She was lifted into the familiar comforting arms. But as she was carried upstairs, she saw the man below toss a blue and yellow vase at the smiling man, her papa. She sensed her nurse jerk as the vase hit a wall with a CRACK!

Kim woke again, sobbing and unable to stop. Alarmed, Paula scrambled out of the tent to get Adam.

He had wakened when the thunder crashed around them again. He heard Paula calling him and unzipped the tent.

"Adam, it's Kim. She just sitting there, sobbing. She won't stop. I don't think she even knows I'm there."

For a moment, Adam was torn about going, but Kim was his sister.

"I'll go and stay with her. Why don't you stay here with Grant?"

Now it was Paula who wasn't sure.

"Don't do anything I wouldn't do," Adam told them.

"I just want to go to sleep," Paula stated.

Grant said, "I'm good."

Adam thought, you'd better be. If his step-father knew he had let his over 18 year old friend spend part of the night with Kim's 16 year old friend...Adam shuddered and pushed the thought away. Instead, he entered the tent, and Kim threw herself at him, still sobbing, and hiccupping now as well. It had been years since Kim had been as bad as this, but he knew what to do. He felt around for Kim's water bottle, and with his free hand, passed it to her.

"Start sipping that, silly. Unless you want to hiccup until morning."

Kim knew what to do as well. Concentrate on taking small, evenly spaced sips. Shortly, the hiccups stopped and Kim drew a deep breath, the sobs subsiding to just an occasional one.

Now Adam took up the blanket Paula had left, and wrapped it around Kim and himself. Her wold creature-like movements next to him, roused some very inappropriate reactions in him. He hoped Kim wouldn't notice. "What's the matter? Is it just the storm?"

"No, I mean yes, a bit but I had a truly awful dream. Holder me tighter, please Adam."

"Tell me about the dream," Adam asked her. He had tightened

his hug, but not by much.

"I was on the stairs, looking down. A man was shouting. He threw a vase..." Kim stopped. The vision was replaying, but this time she saw a knife being thrown. "...a knife. It could have killed the other man. The one who usually smiled at me."

"The other man, who was he?" Adam prompted.

"The same man I saw by the river."

"It's just a dream," Adam said.

"No! The knife just missed him."

"There is no one there now, Kim. You're safe. I think it was Bennett turning up that frightened you. He's harmless."

Kim shook her head, insistent. "It wasn't a dream. I saw it."

Adam didn't push it. All Kim's dreams were vividly real to her. She buried her head on his shoulder, as another thunder clap rent the air. That one must have ripped the clouds as well, for heavy rain started to fall, threatening to collapse the light weight tent.

A short time later, the tent flap was unzipped and opened. A very wet Paula crawled into the tent followed by an even wetter Grant.

"Sorry to make it so cosy," Grant said. "The other tent collapsed."

"More the merrier," Adam told him, relieved on more than one level.

HOLDER OF SECRETS 2 - UNSUSPECTED
After barely escaping death, Peg Jessup and friend Jack, go north for a new start. Peg's nascent musical talent impels them to Tamworth and leads to a fantastic opportunity. Now called Megan, she learns of shares bequeathed by her mother and the deadly interest of two rival companies. When unwanted attention falls on her, her fledgling career is put in jeopardy. The story is set in the 1970s.

HOLDER OF SECRETS 3 - UNREPENTANT
Targeted by criminals who fear the end of their unopposed reign of terror, the former Peg Jessup, now Megan Dawes, intends to fight back. Odd things revealed by her aunt and items she saved from her aunt's house, give the police new leads to facts that could put the men away for life. The same information provides further surprises about her own origins. The story is set in the early 1970s.

MAEVEN DRAGON THIEF
Running away from an arranged marriage, Princess Maeven decides to become a thief. But was it choice or destiny? For when the kingdom faces grave peril, her skills are needed, and the dying dragon mage has chosen her to protect her successor.

MAEVEN DRAGON AGENT
When Maeven threw herself between her son and the ruthless demon, Ciabolo, her twisty tongue didn't save her. Captured and taken to the citadel of the kingdom's enemies, she uses her skills of thief and spy to learn their secrets.

MAEVEN DRAGON CHAMPION
Maeven wakes to find her body possessed by a powerful demon. Only when he sleeps, can she act - to be a thief and spy within the enemy's citadel. Can her kin oust the demon from her body so she can reveal his weaknesses?

THE TYMOREAN TRUST BOOK 5 – ALIEN CONTACT
Tymos and Kryslie Ward, hide their Tymorean intelligence and abilities while working as low ranked technicians at the WSRA's lunar base. When an alien ship arrives at Lunar One, pursued by a powerful enemy who will stop at nothing to get what he wants, only the two Tymorean Great Ones have the knowledge and abilities to overcome him, but to do so they must risk their sanity, and their souls.

THE TYMOREAN TRUST BOOK 6 – INVASION
Great Ones Tymos and Kryslie go to rescue the crew of Earth's first deep space mission – and discover that Ciriot space pirates have discovered Earth's location. When the Ciriot invade in force, the Great Ones reveal themselves so that Earth can gain vital help. However, Kryslie becomes the victim of Ciriot, who want to control her mind and make her betray the people of Earth.

TRICKS
Tom and Jo Dwyer had a reputation for playing tricks – and getting detention. They didn't seem to care about that, so long as they made their class laugh. That was until someone began to turn their tricks against them, and it was no longer funny.

THE CHANCE TO BE ME
Orphan Brenda Jacobs finds herself travelling to a strange town to spend the summer holidays, but trouble finds her there and the actions of her relatives make her life seem bleak. Then an unexpected discovery totally changes her future.

THE MAGPIE'S DAUGHTER
Andy is almost 18 and free of her brother. Outwardly honest, Martin was really a crook, but she didn't dare prove it. When she runs away, Martin comes after her. Owing money, he wants her inheritance. What can Andy do when his enemies find her?

HOLDER OF SECRETS 1 - UNREGARDED
Just out of a girl's training centre, 17 YO Peg Jessup returns home to rural Victoria. Loath to be sent back, and unwilling to be bullied, Peg decides to straighten out her aunt. In the process, she learns of her aunt's relationship to dangerous men, and oddities about her own origins. When the men realise her aunt had kept secrets from them, Peg also becomes a target. The story is set in the 70s.

ATAPI SORCERESS
Jai Cassidy is beginning her mission of reversing the decline of the non-humanoid Atapi. As a sorceress and an Atapi-Human hybrid, she is vehemently disliked by the male Atapi sorcerers and the humanoid rulers of Korvu. Her task is complicated by the treachery of a group of alien engineers, who are inciting insurrection and harsh reprisals.

THE TYMOREAN TRUST BOOK 1 - POWER RISING
The Tymorean Trust - When peace rules Tymorea - Peace reigns in the universe.
Chosen to be the Advocates of the mystical and incorporeal Guardians of Peace, twins Tymos and Kryslie must first learn to control and use the power rising in them - or it will destroy them.
On Tymorea, only the ruling Triumvirate Governors are powerful enough to guide the strong-willed alien-bred twins until they have mastered their power.

THE TYMOREAN TRUST BOOK 2 - GREAT ONES
The peace of the Guardian Planet, Tymorea, is in deadly peril. War there will create ripples of unrest and destruction throughout the settled universe. Tymos and Kryslie, still adolescents, have barely mastered their power and Llaimos is still less than a year old, but they are the three chosen to be Advocates of the mystical Guardians of Peace, to safeguard the Tymorean Trust.

THE TYMOREAN TRUST BOOK 3 - RETURN TO EARTH
Even before the war on Tymorea, the Elders foresaw that Great Ones Tymos and Kryslie would have an imperative mission on Earth.
But as the Tymoreans prepare to build an Earthbase to support them, they discover that specifications for two vital protective shields are missing.
Now, nearly a century later, Tymos and Kryslie must find his work and build the generator before the base is found.

THE TYMOREAN TRUST BOOK 4 - EARTH MISSION
Just before their graduation from the prestigious WSRA Washington University, Tymos and Kryslie Ward deliberately disappear.
The Great Ones have foreseen the capture and death of the new Tymorean missionaries and discovered that the leader of the Eastern Imperium plans to undermine the United World Nations.
Tymos and Kryslie must protect their kin and prevent a potentially devastating world war.

THE SERPENT'S SHADOW
Three books in one.
Janna consorts with terrorists to protect her friend Prince Ali from assassins.
Former cyber-criminal, Erin, becomes part of the merchandise of stolen tech secrets.
Jim Phillip's team is sent to neutralise the leader of the terrorist Cobra Sect.

ROYAL FAVOUR
A quick in-out investigation by US State Department agent, Wanda Martin, is compromised when she is caught after an illicit survey of an ultra-private club. When she should have been gone, team leader Jim Phillips, must organise medical help for her serious wounds as well as adapting his plans to thwart a traitor wishing to turn a tiny European Kingdom into a haven for international crooks

FOREIGN AGENT - THIEF
When US Trade Consul, Allan Wexford, and his daughter go missing, Wanda Martin flies to Austria to find them. Operating on her own, using old and new skills, she begins to unobtrusively unravel Wexford's movements. In spite of all her skill, she becomes a person of interest to both the police and a group of violent criminals, and she is set up to take the fall for a heinous crime.

PRISONER - SPY
On remand for murders she didn't commit and a robbery she never intended to do, Wanda Martin tries to keep from thinking of the inevitable outcome. Yet it is soon apparent that the Russian crime family, whose plans she wrecked, want revenge, and even in prison she isn't safe.

KORVU: THE BEGINNING
Jai Ansuni was the first female Atapi sorcerer for thousands of years, but she dare not reveal it. However, when tribal sorcerer, Stacion Ansuni escalates the enmity between Atapi and Kumatan to an ominous level. Jai and her womb mate, Con, try to mitigate his atrocities but can two young Atapi, not even a score of years old, win against the powerful sorcerer?

THE WILD ONE
Sixteen year old Jai Cassidy thought she was finally free of her family until she is discovered by her other relatives...the ones that aren't human. Jai uses her natural perversity and cunning to escape their control, but catapults herself into the middle of a deadly feud between two alien races.

ERIN: THE FORCING OF WISDOM

For years, Erin has used the intricacies of cyberspace to banish unwanted emotions. Others call what she does hacking, and her manipulations criminal, but now her skill was exceptional - in, out, traceless. She was wrong. Someone betrayed her.

Travis has dangerous plans. He needs an electronics expert – one he can coerce through fear. Erin was perfect.

With the inescapable threat of prison looming, Erin accepts his offer of sanctuary. When she realises his intentions, she is in too deep. But the terrifying of innocents is unforgivable. She cannot walk away. She is an empath and shares their distress. She has to help them, even if it means prison, and insanity...

ERIN: THE CALL

(including ELISABETH AND TANYA: BLOOD CALLS TO BLOOD.

Elisabeth's sister, Wanda, had been missing for half a year. Multiple authorities had found no trace of her, or her two colleagues. Yet she knew her sister was still alive and had answered a call for help from an alien who had once lived on Earth.

Elisabeth, along with her newly found cousin Tanya, have started to sense things from her missing sister. Enough to know that she is in dire trouble, but not enough to help her.

While looking for traces of the aliens, Elisabeth makes some unexpected discoveries about her family. Yet even with the help of a second newly discovered cousin, she fears she is not strong enough to help her sister and the others to return.

ERIN: THE CALL

Convicted cyber-criminal, Erin Mason, is startled into awareness in an unfamiliar place, with no memory of escaping and only vague memories of getting there. Voices in her head were urging her to go west, and they were getting more urgent.

After a chance meeting with covert agent, Jim Phillips, when she helped save his mission, he realised that she might be the key to another, more personal quest – to find three missing state department agents.

All he must do is keep Erin safe, and hide her from an intense police search, until he can introduce her to cousins she was unaware of.

However her uncontrolled psychic gifts conflict with a logical mind that prefers the ordered intricacies of computers and electronics. She only wants to shut out the voices and the madness she sees looming.

Can Phillips convince her to help him, before the forces of the law find her?

"And Kim, I think I understand your concerns. Maybe you should ask your stepfather, about changing schools. Janice said that Paula is your only real friend. At a new school, you can make new friends who will only know you as Kathy Ryman and won't find a boyfriend named Adam Laurensen to be anything to comment about."

"I won't change my mind," Kim vowed.

'Nor I," Adam echoed.

Grace smiled at them. She decided if they were still so sure when Kim was older, their bond would be even stronger. And if not, they would still be the closest of friends. She stood up, leaving them to think over what she said.

"It will be hard," Adam said, reaching out a hand to Kim's. "But, it is the best way. I won't say I won't go out with girls while I am away, but you will be the only one I want to keep seeing forever. Any others will be camouflage."

"I will be waiting," Kim told him. "And as soon as I am eighteen, our life will start."

"It's a promise," Adam agreed, giving her a hug and a quick kiss on the top of her head.

The End.

"When I took you away, it was only meant to be for a short time. So I took you to my sister's place. No one was meant to know about you because Marcus was already aware of trouble. I won't go into all that. Some of it has become public record now. The thing was, people knew I worked for your parents, and should someone come looking for me, as Bray did, it wouldn't have been safe for Kim to be with me. Janice had just lost a child and her husband. You were like a gift from heaven. Someone who needed her. You, Adam, you missed your father. And like your mother, you knew Kim needed you."

"How does this help," Adam asked, helplessly.

"Let me finish," Grace asked. "Janice felt the need to join the church. The people hadn't known her before, so they accepted her as a widow with two children. She made friends and that was another layer of protection for you, Kim. She met and agreed to marry Jeremiah. He was what she needed, and she does love him. Again though, he was another formidable protector. Until recently, she had not told him the truth regarding you. He truly believed you were brother and sister."

"He knows now, but –" Adam began, but Grace silenced him with a look.

"My sister never formally adopted you, neither did Jeremiah. Yes, she chose to use his name when you started school. Kim is now able to use her legal identity. Yes, you grew up together, but in fact you are merely foster sibs."

"Not everyone who knows of me will hear who I really am," Kim said.

"The problem you have now, is the age difference. Until Adam turned 18, and left you behind as a minor, there was no issue. Kim, you will be 18 in a year and a half. It might seem like a lifetime, but it will pass quickly. Adam, have you decided what you will do next year?"

Adam told her what courses he had applied for.

"Then what I think you should consider doing is to go and live on campus, or in the city. Time away from each other will enable you to be sure of what you feel. If you are meant to be together, it is worth waiting for it. At least think about it."

"All right," Adam agreed.

Chapter 31: A Promise for the Future

Grace found Kim sitting by herself in the lounge and settled herself nearby.

"Why do I feel you are glad for so many people, but sad for yourself? Is just because of all that has happened?"

"It's that, I suppose," Kim answered, but it wasn't all.

"Is there still something on your mind? I am willing to listen to you without judging you."

Needing to share how she felt, with someone, her one time nurse and current well-loved aunt, was probably the perfect ear.

She started slowly, telling her aunt how she felt about Adam and how she had come to understand it wasn't allowed. As she finished all she had to say, Adam knocked on the doorframe. Grace gestured him in.

"Kim loves you. Do you know that?" Grace introduced the subject, and pointed to a place to sit.

Adam didn't know how to answer. "I love her too, of course," was his careful answer.

"Just like a sister?" Grace prompted.

"No...more than that," Adam admitted quietly. "We know now, that we are not blood siblings, but people will still think we are, and if we become a couple they will point at us."

"How is your step-father taking this?"

Adam's expression betrayed what he didn't say.

"He is a good man," Grace stated. "He treats my sister well, and took you both in and provided a good home, and what you needed."

"I know that, and I have come to understand him better. It can't be easy to stick to doing the right thing. The morally right thing. I used to hate him, but particularly now, when the example of Bray is in everyone's mind, I would rather be more like him."

"And that's the real conflict," Grace murmured, and for a while she seemed to be thinking.

"My sister suspected how you felt about each other, and even though she knew the truth about Kim, chose to abide with Jeremiah's beliefs. Maybe I can explain."

Adan leant forward, hoping for a slice of hope.

"I've grown up being taught to earn what I want by hard work. I can't imagine wanting to just laze around."

"You've got the right of it," Eugene agreed. "And having family helps too."

The went back to Aunt Grace's house where they were all staying, and told her about their visit to Eugene Bennett.

"The local paper published a statement that his name has been officially cleared of any involvement in the disappearance. All public records and police records will be adjusted to say that."

"That's a good thing," Kim said, not sounding positive. Grace saw a similar sadness in Adam. She decided to find a time to talk to them alone.

"Do you know, Bray tried to convince me that Elena had cheated on Marcus, with you, so that I wasn't Marcus's daughter?" The comment distracted Eugene. "I knew he was lying, but I wouldn't have hated it if you were my father."

"If you had been my daughter, I would have been so proud of you." His eyes were beginning to water, and Kim went and gave him a hug. A moment later, Paula hugged his other side, realising this moment was a long overdue emotional release.

"If you do the house up," Kim went on, not commenting on the tear wracking him. "I want to help. I have been told I am going to be rich, but that doesn't seem real. Even though my stepfather has hired a lawyer to take care of the specifics. If I can, when it's all sorted, I'd like to help you renovate."

"It's a sweet offer, but I was doing it for the wrong reason."

"Then find a new reason," Kim suggested logically. "Maybe make it a place where people can come when they have lost families and need a quiet place to heal. They will know that you understand. Maybe Imogen Kingsley might come to live here. She is likely to be allowed to leave the care home, and has nowhere to go."

"Are you trying to solve everyone's sadness?" Eugene asked. "You are so like your mother."

"I doubt I can help everyone, but those Bray affected deserve a new chance at happy. And, I did bring something for you," Kim added. "I had a copy made of a photo I had of my parents. I know it has both of them in it, but I thought you would like to have it."

Kim and Paula eased away from Eugene as his shaking eased.

"I don't resent Marcus," Eugene said, his eyes filling again. He is part of you, and you seem like family. The only people in a long time who look past what I was."

Adam, moved by the man's words, said, "You are welcome to consider the four of us as family. An extra uncle to keep tabs on Kim wouldn't go amiss."

"You thinking she will give all her money away?" Eugene managed to ask.

"I'm thinking people will want her to be..." Adam didn't finish his thought. He hadn't expected the surge of jealousy that suffused him. Other guys wanting to be her new best friend.

"And you are not interested in her fortune?" Eugene asked.

"I guess the old house rightfully belongs to you now?" Eugene said without emotion.

"I suppose sorting everything out will take time," Kim told him. "And really, I don't want it. I have some memories of my parents there, happy and smiling. I have more that still give me nightmares."

"What happened to Elena gives me sleepless nights. If only I'd known where that ba...where Bray had sent them. I warned them about him, but he still convinced them he was looking out for them, when he was really looking out for himself."

"He is not going to escape jail time," Grant said.

"He'll probably try to convince the other inmates to bow to him," Adam muttered.

Eugene nodded at that. "Prison isn't a pleasant place. Those believed to have money, have it easier. But I did hear his fortune was confiscated."

"So it ought to be," Paula muttered. "I bet he was using Marcus's money to make himself rich."

Adam growled in agreement.

Eugene made a sound like a rusty chuckle. "I made friends in jail. Even though most advice says to avoid them, I know some who tried to stay good after they came out. Some of those just couldn't. I keep in touch and try to encourage them. I sent Tommy Otto a present, when it seemed I was no longer under a cloud. He had a strange way of looking at the world, and he gave me the courage to face each day, then and after. He told me when I spoke to him last by phone, that there will be a fitting welcome for Bray when he gets there."

"A very fitting welcome that is ongoing?" Paula asked hopefully.

Eugene nodded. "I had to go to the city. Had to testify to a few things. While they were there, they read extracts from a journal they say they found with Elena. That Bastard, pardon my French, wrote down what he had done to them. Like he was documenting a process for converting a building for another use. It was sickening."

"He will likely be in jail for the rest of his life," Kim predicted. "You've got the rest of your life to live as you like. Are you going to do the house up?"

"I'm not so sure now. I wanted it, so I could think about her, Elena."

never make up for her losing her daughter, and missing out on watching her granddaughter grow up.

Imogen was still living at the care home, for her house had been sold to pay for her care. Yet as each week passed, her mind grew clearer, as the drugs being used to make her easier to control had been stopped.

No one doubted Kim's relationship to Imogen, so even the DNA proof was an anti-climax. However, she was surprised when she saw the result for each of her parents, until Amherst explained the police had found and kept hair samples from the house when her parents had first gone missing.

At home, Jeremiah Laurensen had made an edict that news reports on the trial, which was dragging on, would be banned. Kim just wanted it to be all over, and was dreading returning to school for the new term. Torn between wanting Bray to suffer, and dreading hearing of his attempts to avoid blame, she had become almost as silent as she used to be. Neither his advice, nor her mother's concern, helped at all.

It was Adam who broke through the silence.

"We should visit Eugene Bennett. Let him know he's been vindicated."

Kim had immediately perked up, and glanced at her step-father for permission.

"That is a very thoughtful gesture, Adam. I think a break from here would be good for you both. I am sure your friends would be glad to go with you."

Eugene Bennett was out the back of his cabin, sanding a stool carved from a log. He walked around to the front to greet them, then invited them around the back.

"I've heard you have been vindicated," Kim said.

"So they say," Eugene agreed. "It doesn't quite seem real yet. And I still feel I failed your mother."

"You did what you could. Bray was just a cold blooded...," Kim didn't want to utter the word that came to mind.

Grant wasn't so restrained. "He was a right greedy, arrogant bastard."

Chapter 30: Justice at Last

A media frenzy erupted with the news of the arrest of Duncan Bray for Murder. As the days passed, rumours of embezzlement and corruption increased as old crimes were exposed. Many of his former and current confederates were arrested, and questioned. In many cases the people were released because of statutes of limitation applied, though reputations were ruined.

Privately, Amherst told Kim and her family, that Westfalls Investments was a cleverly created shell company that laundered money Bray had embezzled from clients.

Grant, Adam, Paula and Kim had shared all they had found with the police. And, from Marcus's journal, they had located the cash missing from Marcus's early accounts. He had transferred all cash assets to a new account, not in his name, but in that of his daughter. It was in a trust that Kim would get access to when she was 21. He had indeed made a new will, though Kim had not known that for sure when she challenged Bray.

Amherst had suggested things to say to Bray which he had hoped to provoke an admission of guilt. Marcus had been aware of inconsistencies in his financial affairs, and had not wanted to believe it was Bray, but his, 'Could it be Bray?' at the end of his journal suggested he thought of it.

Kim began to suspect Amherst had decoded the cryptic journal entries, when he had said about clauses in the will. The will presented for probate was being re-examined. The charities who were to receive bequests if he died with no heirs, were all administered by a company controlled by Bray. Still, he had covered all bases in case questions arose about Elena pre deceasing her husband. Imogen Kingsley's lawyer found it was no longer as he remembered her dictating it. She had known of Kin, or rather Kathy and had not changed it, even after her daughter went missing. To make her wishes absolutely clear, he had advised her to update it, and thanks to her new medication, she could prove she was in her right mind.

Kim made a routine to visit her each Sunday, though it would

Kim was safe. '

His father's common model black sedan had a police guard. The officer opened the back door for him. He helped Kim in then slid into the seat after her. When no one could see them, their mutual relief went past what Adam allowed himself. When their step-father returned, they had a normal space between them.

don't believe Bray."

Bray leant across the table and grabbed her wrist. "You will get nothing! Your father got too interested in matters that weren't his business. He ruined several lucrative deals I was working on. I only took what should have been mine."

"So you killed them," Kim told him, meeting his eyes now, while hiding the pain of his grip.

"There is no way I can be connected to that."

"No?" Kim took a photo of the old ID in front of him. He glanced down. She didn't have to say where it was found.

"Let my hand go," Kim said clearly, relieved to see Amherst close behind Bray.

"No one will believe a lying little witch like you."

"No matter, if they do or don't. The police haven't told me much, and you just ran out of time to make private amends."

The heavy hand on his shoulder, surprised Bray and he released his grasp. Kim pulled her wrist free, stood and walked away. Not once looking back. Not even when a fierce scuffle broke out behind her.

Ahead were her friends – Adrian, Paula, Grant. Her step-father was there as well. She made it to Adam just as the reaction set in. Paula caught her, enough for Adam to slip in and support her other side. Kim revived a bit and turned the support into a hug. Adam took over, when Paula slipped out.

"I'll see what Grant is doing."

Kim remembered to stop her phone recording, and turn off the wiretap. Adam had lightly kissed the top of her head before Kim said, "He's coming over."

Adam felt his face heat up, wondering if his step-father had seen what he had done.

"Do you need to stay here?" Adam asked as Jeremiah Laurensen came close enough to hear. It seemed he needed have worried.

"Help your sister back to the car," Jeremiah told Adam in a mild tone. "I wish to learn what will happen to that evil man."

Adam realised his step-father didn't look angry, not even like he was holding it in check. Maybe he believed it was simple relief that

"Where is this conversation going, you little brat? I can have you thrown in jail for extortion."

"I am only interested in getting my rightful inheritance. You should be interested in making sure all of your clients don't hear about this not so little mistake."

"Your father's estate was distributed to various charities as per his will. I told you, you were not mentioned."

"I have a copy of a will where I am mentioned," Kim lied.

"And what is the date on that will?"

Kim estimated a date.

"The will in my possession was dated six months before they disappeared."

"The will I have, has a specific clause that states that any subsequent will must include a clause confirming my disposition."

"That will is obviously a forgery. Do you have it with you?"

"No." Kim told him. She decided his next comment would determine the outcome.

"Where did you find someone to forge it?"

"I am not even sure how to make a will," Kim lied again. Her step-father had ensured she now had a valid will, though until it was suggested, she had given the idea no thought. "However, the way the will I have was located was from his journal. That book had a summary of his financial affairs, bank accounts, shares and their value, and who to contact about his will, and that was dated a month after my birth. "

"The one I had was three years newer," Bray insisted.

"So, where did you find someone to forge it?" Kim threw his comment back at him. The tick in his cheek was going even faster.

"Now, if you don't want it known you extorted my father's estate –"

"You little witch. You won't get away with this. There is nothing for you. The estate was wound up."

"Actually, that is not true," Kim surprised him. "When you presented the will for probate, all his bank accounts were inexplicably empty."

"Your father must have done that."

"Why? You said he didn't believe he was in danger," Kim challenged him. "Though I know he finally figured you out. The last thing he wrote in his journal was, 'If something happens to me,

"My dear, I was so sorry to hear about you parents."

"So you now realise I was telling you the truth," Kim was not quite meeting his eyes, a deliberate ploy Amherst had suggested.

"Yes, and I have learnt you are not 18, as you claimed."

"And my parents did not race of to get me when they didn't go to the cabin you told the police you sent them to," Kim commented in return. She glanced at him and saw the twitch in his cheek.

"Does your guardian know you are here?" Bray tried to worry her.

"This does not concern him," Kim told him, unruffled.

"So, why did you want to see me?"

"I know things now," Kim told him. Like you looked after my father's financial affairs."

"That is true, I was also executor of his will."

"And had my parents declared dead."

"It was a necessary step," Bray explained.

"Did you advertise for people with..." Kim paused to make it seem she needed to recall something. "...claims on the estate?"

"Naturally. Again, it is part of the process."

"I'm told my parents died at the same time," Kim related. "And in those cases, the elder is deemed to have died first. The younger inherits the estate."

"You have been misinformed. The police have records of you parents accessing accounts. Your father continued accessing his accounts long after your mother did. She still had money in her account."

"They were found together in a cabin you once owned. As executor, you settled the estate incorrectly. Were you also executor for my mother's estate?"

"Your mother had few assets."

"Not if you did your job correctly," Kim accused, with a hint of a threat. "And even if, as you tried to tell me, my mother cheated on my father, his estate rightly belongs to me."

"Elena's estate went to her mother!"

"Who is a sick woman, who now accepts I am her grandchild."

"And should she change it now, any competent lawyer will claim she was coerced, tricked, or not in her right mind."

"Actually," Kim said, easing her tone. "She has been a lot better since we met. Even her doctor says so."

Chapter 29: Confronting a Killer

Kim wanted to kick everything. Amherst was keeping her up to date with the new investigation, and even with the glaring evidence, Bray had answers for everything, and neatly shifted all blame to Eugene Bennett.

So far, the police forensic experts hadn't been able to separate pages of the book found under Elena's remains. The identities of the two skeletons had been confirmed and their time of death estimated. And that had opened a whole new can of worms. One that disproved the belief that Elena had died before Marcus. The matter of the distribution of Marcus's estate was now under intense scrutiny. She hoped Bray was shivering in his designer label shoes, and running out of logical sounding arguments.

"I wish he'd let me go face to face with him," Kim growled. "I would twist him up in his own lies."

It seemed like the fates heard her.

"Are you sure about this?" Adam asked, his concern evident.

"Yes!" Kim stated with conviction. "Amherst hasn't mentioned the ID, but I can bring that up. Plus stuff we figured out. I will have my phone recording and one of the police gadgets."

"What makes you think he won't just kill you?" Adam revealed his worst fear.

"That's one reason why I am meeting him in a public place. There will be plain clothed police nearby and they will hear what I'm saying. I will also have a help phrase, and if they lose contact, they will move in. Besides, Bray has been checking on me. He thinks our step-dad is an ogre, that I am still cloudy brained, and I am still very timid. He won't know about my memory now."

"Well, I don't like it."

"I know," Kim said with sympathy. Her heart ached for him, wanted to reassure him more personally and have it returned.

Adam watched her enter the café, and sent a silent prayer skywards.

Kim made her way to where Bray sat, after telling the girl greeter she was meeting her grandfather.

It all took time, and it was mid-afternoon when the coroner was able to examine the first skeleton, in situ.

About the same time, DI Amherst arrived on the scene. The senior constable reported all they knew.

The first skeleton was female. With the help of Grant's device, they found the second.

Amherst glanced at Kim, when the officer asked about looking for an infant's remains. He had heard the couple believed to be there had become parents.

"Senior constable, I see my message was misunderstood. If these are indeed the remains of Marcus and Elena Ryman, then we have their child and her friends to thank for finding them."

Kim became the target for the officer's scrutiny, since Amherst had an arm across her shoulders.

"You should really leave us to do our job here," he told her when the officer returned to his task.

"What about Bray?" Kim asked.

Amherst patted her shoulder. "He believes he is helping us to understand this find. How did you decide to look here?"

She twisted to Grant, who came closer to explain.

"I see. What other information do you have?"

"Um...I have a journal that was once Marcus's. It's back at home," Kim admitted, flushing.

"At a more comfortable time and place, I need to find out all you know," Amherst murmured.

The police photographer took another flash photo.

"Sir?" Someone called over.

With a brief instruction to stay out of the way, Amherst went to see what was found. It was now in a plastic bag, but from Kim's vantage point, it looked like a book. The others agreed.

for the offending object. She felt something around her ankle, and pulled on it. It wasn't wood.

"Huh! Someone's ID," Kim guessed. She took it from Paula and really looked at it. "Oh, my...." She glanced back at the cabin, suddenly silent.

Paula took the plasticised card from Kim's limp hand. "Sheesh, it was him." Then she too glanced at the collapsed cabin and realised the boys were acting oddly.

"What should I do with this?" Paula asked.

Kim, trance broken, said, "I'll take a photo. Put it back down in the grass, too. Look for a way to pinpoint it. I've an idea. Go get Adam."

Adam's face paled when he took the photo. "You need to give Amherst a call."

"Wh...what did you find?" Kim asked.

"I think they are here. Marcus and Elena."

Kim tried to run to Grant, but Adam caught her. "You won't see anything. Grant had a kind of camera on a flexible lead he could push into cracks. So send Amherst the photo of that, and tell him Grant will send a video."

With fingers that trembled so much it was hard to press the buttons, Kim sent her photo, and the message Adam had suggested. She told Grant Amherst's phone number. A message came back quickly. "Send GPS cords."

"How do I do that?" Kim asked helplessly. Adam took her phone and sent the phones location to Amherst's number.

"Stay there. Help on the way," was the next reply.

Ten minutes later, the rumble of a powerful motorbike could be heard coming closer.

"It's too soon for someone to come from town," Gavin said. "I know he said stay, but grab your stuff. We should get out of sight."

"I wonder what fell on that," Adam remarked with an attempt at humour. There was no sign that a big bough had fallen to collapse the cabin, but that's what it looked like. The log walls had collapsed, coming apart where the sides joined, though the chimney still stood tall and defiant. The rustic style porch had the former overhang covering it.

"Look around," Adam suggested to the girls. He and Grant moved closer to the collapsed structure.

"The wood is rotting," Grant noted.

"Come look here," Adam pointed. "Looks like someone swung a sledge hammer at it."

Grant took a photo with a small digital camera, then stepped back to get the overall picture. They continued circling the remains, until Grant decided to step carefully on the outer logs, to get a closer look at the centre.

He called out in a quieter voice, "Part of this wood is burnt."

"So someone might have had a fire going?" Adam suggested.

"I agree, but I have a nasty feeling," Grant abruptly admitted. "Can you pass me something? In the smaller compartment of my pack there is a black zip up pouch."

Adam knelt beside Grant's bag and when he found the item, he asked, "What is it?"

"It's a long flexible tube with a fish eye lens and a light at one end. The other end can connect to my phone and send images. I'm going to poke it down between stuff and see if I can pick up anything."

Kim and Paula watched what the boys were doing as they circled the wrecked cabin at a wider distance, swishing through long grass.

"I don't know what they think we will find around here," Paula grumbled. "And Grant had better be careful. If he's not he might put his foot in a hole and get it stuck."

She wasn't paying attention to the ground and unexpectedly tripped and fell.

"Are you okay?" Kim asked rushing over to help her up. "Are you hurt?"

"Only my pride." Paula tried to brush it off. "My foot caught on something, probably a dead branch."

As she pushed herself to a kneeling position, she felt around

"Will I still be able to visit her?" Kim asked.

"I am hoping that you will. The doctor thinks it will help her."

"Then, I will. That's okay isn't it?" Kim looked at her step-father.

"It is indeed a Christian thing to do," he replied evenly.

"And it would be useful if you recorded your meetings in case you provoke some useful memories."

"Ok, I will. Do you have a business card or something?"

Amherst opened a card holder and passed her one. "You can call me any time," he invited.

"Are you going to look into those old events again?"

"The case involving your parents is still open. I have requested authority to reactivate it. I expect there will be no dissent."

When Amherst had left, Kim's step-father remarked, "You will of course, not bother him needlessly."

Kim was full of excitement at being allowed to go back to Twin Falls. It was decided that the two girls, since Paula was going as well, would stay with Grace Westcott, while Adam and Grant planned to rent one of the cabins for the week.

When Grant spoke to Hal Taylor, the old man murmured word that someone had wanted to know about him. In answer to Grants question of who, Hal had only said, "You had the right of it."

When they arrived, Hal drove out to the cabin they were using to give them the keys. Grant intended to keep a low profile. He and Adam, along with the girls had agreed they needed to check out the four places as soon as they could. They hoped a week would be long enough.

They each had a hiking pack with the usual food, water and necessities, but Grant had brought along a number of items he hadn't mentioned to the others. He made sure they all had a GPS app on their phones, with their targets as dot points, and they had discussed contingencies.

The first two days proved fruitless. The two cabins still stood, but had obviously been left to the depredations of time and the elements. The third, when they saw it had all of them stopping well back from it.

DI Amherst made an unannounced visit the following day, and when Kim heard he was wanting to see her, she was apprehensive for no reason she could determine. She was glad to see her mum and step-father waiting with him. He came straight to the point.

"After your visit to Imogen Kingsley, I made some enquiries. As you are her next of kin, I felt you should be kept aware of developments."

"Have the DNA results come back yet?"

"No, that will take longer than three days. But I have enough data to feel confident you are Kathryn Ryman."

"So what has happened? Is Imogen okay?"

"Yes, I spoke to her personal physician. Your instinct with the tablets was basically correct. He did not authorise the new medication. The in-house physician did, based on observations from the nursing staff. I also received a confidential outline of her medical problems. I won't go into that, but I showed him the photo I took of her medication chart, and the tablets I had in that bag. One look and he was extremely concerned. "

"So...the tablets weren't working?" Kim tried to comprehend what he was saying.

"No, in fact they would be making it worse. He authorised her to be transferred to a private hospital, and he is going to take her off her current medications and re-evaluate her."

"I don't understand," Kim admitted. She looked at Amherst while he carefully explained what the doctor had told him.

"So, someone wanted her to fade into obscurity," Kim finally summarised.

"Something like that. Her doctor thinks she will actually improve with time and care. Meanwhile, I have started an investigation into the care home, keeping it low key as the place does have a really good reputation otherwise. I am also looking into who is administering her financial affairs. I'm told her stay there is being financed by her estate. Also, I checked some dates. Her apparent early onset dementia occurred only a few years after her daughter vanished. Before that she was insisting her daughter had to be still alive."

The police officer with a senior constable's insignia, asked, "You found remains here?"

"Yes. I had a gadget that I can poke into places to see what's there," Grant admitted. He received a sharp look, but he went on to say, "I can show you what it picked up, from about where the centre of the roof is."

"What were you young people doing here in the first place?"

"Looking around," Adam told him. "We weren't exactly looking for...that sort of remains. Just for places that might have lodged some missing people."

"What made you think you'd find such a police, when the police back then couldn't?"

Kim blurted, "They can't have looked here."

"And why are you so interested?"

"Because Imogen Kingsley deserves to know what happened to her daughter."

The man in brown, who was in the uniform of the forest service, commented, "This place wasn't being rented back then."

Kim ignored that as a stupid comment. "There is something else," she said turning her attention to the senior constable. "We left it where we found it."

One of the constables was directed to come over. Paula went with Kim to where they had left the ID card with its foot trapping lanyard. Kim pointed to the plastic coated ID of a 12 years younger Duncan Bray."

It was in the grass. Paula caught her foot in it and tripped."

The card was carefully placed in a plastic evidence bag.

Grant finished showing where his camera had shown him the outline of bones and allowed one of the officers to see the video. He was then asked by the man in black, who introduced himself as the local coroner, if he could have the use of the camera gadget.

After that, Grant moved out of the way, to where his friends waited. Kim flatly refused to go back down to where grant had parked his car. So they watched as the police and park ranger first photographed the scene, then began to remove pieces of the fallen cabin – the metal roof, and fallen logs.

Chapter 28

Grant hid behind a wide tree trunk and had a narrow field of view back towards the cabin. Two heavy set men now stalked around the cabin. He had managed to get a photo of one of them.

"I thought this place burnt down," one said. His voice carrying in the stillness.

"Obviously, it didn't," his mate growled. "Someone must have come here, but I can't see any signs."

That voice stopped, then spoke like he had called someone. "No one around. No signs anyone was. But the place never burnt...how the hell do you think that will look? Fine, but it will draw attention. Likely to spread to the forest." The man then cursed, most likely after the call ended.

"He reckons to burn the place. He's nuts."

"Everything is still damp from that storm last week. How does he think...? We could empty some fuel from the bike."

"Then let's do it and get the hell away."

Grant quickly sent Amherst a text, "Two men to burn cabin."

A moment later, sirens could be heard, and the two men had an urgent argument. "Do it and run" against "Let's just get away from here."

The sound of the bike stating up and roaring away, proved the winner.

Grant told the others to wait, even after seeing and hearing a group of six people crossing his line of sight. His phone vibrated. Amherst's number showed on his screen. He answered and heard, "Where are you?"

"Hiding from the two blokes who took off on a big motorbike."

"Has the team arrived?"

"Yes. A guy in brown, six flashy police types and a guy in black."

"I will let them know you will go see them." Amherst ended the call, and a phone rang nearby.

Grant whistled quietly and gestured when they came into view. They all walked down together to meet the police responders.

of the cabins he rents out.”

“Would they check everyone who wants to rent a cabin?” Kim asked.

“Doesn’t seem logical,” Adam decided. “Unless they felt someone was looking for something, someone didn’t want found.”

“Like Bray. Since I went and saw him and he discovered the Rymans had a child,” Kim shuddered.

“Hard to believe a guy like him would have done something shady,” Adam had to say. “So, if he has done underhanded things, he’s good at hiding the traces.”

“Do you know where those few cabins are?” Kim wanted to know.

“Not exactly.”

“So if we have to wait until the stuff arrives, what else can we do?”

“I can see if Murph has had any more luck with Marcus’s journal,” Grant proposed.

“Or Kim and I finish our house arrest and seem to have lost interest,” Adam said without looking at Kim.

When Grant turned to other topics, Kim went back to her room to continue a project she had started, which was writing down everything she recalled about her parents and what she had learnt about that life.

sent some envelopes to himself, and they would be coming in a parcel from her sister. She promised to have Adam call him when they arrived.

When they were finally alone, Grant gave in to the, "Tell us!" command from his friends.

"Well, starting with Bray. He told the police he had sent the Rymans to a cabin he rented occasionally. Hal, the guy I spoke to up there, said he hadn't handled the rentals for the big money clients. So that cut out a lot of the rental places up there. The particular one Bray must have mentioned to the police, was looked at and there had been no sign of anyone having gone there. Hal got the other guy's old records when he retired. A lot of the other guy's clients went over to Hal. I was assuming we could rule out any of those that have been rented out regularly since then. I also found out Bray has his own cabin, and is a stickler about privacy."

"Would he have..." Kim began. "I was going to say, sent them there and lied about the other place."

"I won't rule that out," Gavin said seriously. "Hal also said, there are still a number of privately owned cabins. I don't know if they are still used or not, He doesn't have a list of those. However, going through those old records, I noticed a number that were once owned by Bray, but were sold to Westfalls Investments. Most of those are still being rented regularly. However, a few of Conroy's former rentals haven't been rented out for years. Hal let me take the files of four that caught my attention. He doesn't need to keep them any longer. The ones he took on to manage, he began new files and the rest he no longer needs. He only needed to keep them for seven years, and could have got rid of them years ago."

"So, what caught your attention?" Adam asked.

"Mainly that the last time they were rented out was about when the Rymans vanished. I didn't look back beyond that."

"So we have to wait to go through those files," Kim sighed.

"Do you think we should look at those places?" Adam asked.

"It can't hurt. Worst result, we won't find anything," Grant shrugged.

"But you think someone saw you and checked up on you?" Kim remarked. "Why would they do that?"

"I can only think it was because Hal was showing me a number he thought of Hal's late visitor, wouldn't have found anything useful in his car or his pack. He had deliberately left that in the car, as if implying there was nothing to find, or he was totally naïve. It had to be that someone was covering all bases. He felt sure Hal would not he had files, or even that they had been out. That reminded him to call Hal, and say he had to return home, but would be in touch when he got back there.

After getting a snack to go, Grant left the service station and continued on his way. He had no sense of being followed, but still breathed easier once he was home.

Adam answered Grant's call and demanded, "What kept you?"

"This and that. I am to tell you your aunt is sending your mum a parcel."

"What's in it?"

"Some kind of throw rug, I think. If you mum doesn't know about it, likely there will be a letter with it."

"Fine! Did you find what you went for?"

"Does your house arrest include no visitors?" Grant asked instead of answering the question.

"I think it's just no internet," Adam growled.

"How did Kim's visit go?"

"She and the old lady got on really well. Are you coming around?"

"Ten minutes."

Jeremiah Laurensen, didn't refuse the visitor. He had obviously come to the conclusion that Kim wanted to know more about her birth parents, and her friends and brother were helping her.

Added to that, Amherst had been very impressed by how well Kim had treated Imogen Kingsley. Not only that, casual comments she had made had been insightful.

Though there was more that he didn't mention. The sudden sense of danger to the woman, now she had met Kim.

Grant was asked to wait in the lounge, while Jeremiah went it summon Adam and Kim. He still considered them as family. However, he didn't stay to overhear their conversation. Adam's mum came in to offer refreshments, and Grant explained he had

Grace hurried off, and Grant began to remove all the pages from one folder. When the envelopes came, he transferred them to one, and Grace helped with the remaining folders. Grant addressed each envelope to himself, care of the post office nearest his home.

"If you give them to me, I can take them to the post office tomorrow," Grace offered.

"That should be fine," Grant said, then thought he should add, "Hal let me have them, but some guy turned up that gave me a few shivers."

"Are they urgent?"

"Not really."

"Don't lose any sleep. I have a place to keep them where no one will think to look. When I next go to town, I will take a small rug with me that I plan to send to my sister. Anyone who sees me, will see that and not what will be hidden inside it."

Grant grinned. "I like the way you think."

"Now, come along. I have put some towels in my spare room."

Grant left early, but even so, his hostess had cooked him breakfast and wouldn't accept payment for food or board. She even came out to see him off as if he was family.

When he first opened his car, Grant thought he smelt cigarette smoke. He glanced at his bag and thought that had been gone through, but he said nothing, just headed off.

As he drove down the road, he watched to see if anyone was paying him attention. After half an hour, during which he saw no car that seemed to be following him, he told himself to stop being paranoid. Only when he stopped for a break, did he check his bag on the pretext of getting out his water bottle. Close up, the bag did have the same smoky odour. He checked his sketch books and found dusty smudges on the corner of a couple of pages, like someone had flicked through them.

"Not totally paranoid," Grant said in a low voice, to himself. "Are they convinced?" He could think of a reason to be anyone's person of interest, unless she had got to close to somewhere...like a cabin... and he wasn't local.

Logically, there was nothing suspicious about anything he did. Unless someone had a seriously guilty conscience. They, and here

Chapter 26: Grant Turns Detective

Grant admitted to having a bad feeling about the newcomer, even though Hal hadn't seemed worried, except for the unexpected visit. He hoped he hadn't seemed too interested in the Ryman mystery, but Hal had intuited his interest, didn't seem to like Bray, and hopefully wouldn't mention the files now in his pack.

He had intended to drive back home, but it was later than he had planned to leave, and he'd had two beers on very little food. He rang his mother, told her he would be staying in Twin Falls for the night. His first thought had been to find a caravan park, then he remembered Adam's aunt.

He rang Adam. "Reckon your aunt would put me up for the night?"

Adam was sure she would and offered to call her. Grant was relieved when Adam called back with, "She'll be expecting you."

After driving around the block to get his bearings, Grant found his way to Grace Westcott's house.

She was plainly happy to see him, and was too polite to ask about the bundle of files he brought in. Grant though was calling himself paranoid for doing it, and leaving his pack in the car. If anyone did break into the car, and looked – one of the sketch pads did have some artistic attempts he'd done on an art trail around the city. They weren't great, but that didn't matter.

"Thanks for putting me up," Grant told Grace. "I had a couple more drinks than usual, and thought it better not to drive back tonight."

"A short trip this time?" Grace commented.

"I'd hoped Adam could get away, but he went and got himself grounded. Him and Kim."

Grace sighed. "So what have you been up to?"

"Looking at rustic cabins. My grandpa used to come up here fishing, and usually stayed at one. I was trying to find out if it still existed." In a lower voice, even though no one would hear him, he asked, "Do you have some large envelopes I can have to post this stuff to myself?"

"I do, and I know just where they are."

a year or two back."

"It was a long shot," Grant said, shrugging. "I suppose, for my purpose, any cabin would do." With that, Grant downed the last of the beer in his can, and left the can on the table. He grabbed his pack and said, "I'll let myself out."

"That would be right wise of you, lad."

They looked at two more cabins before Taylor had to head back to town. Grant had said the only problem with the ones he'd seen were they were too close to the road.

"What say you come round to the shop later and I can point out others that are more out of the way," Taylor invited. "I'll be free about six."

"You're on," Grant agreed, deciding to go find food to pass the time until then.

Once Taylor returned and let him into the shop, he locked the outer door, and grabbed a six pack from a small fridge. He showed Grant to a table and chairs in his office, then wandered off through a door leading off it. He returned with a dusty box. He didn't bother trying to brush dust of the top, just lifted the cover and put it aside. "Only used this stuff to check details for the places that came over to me. Not all of them did. If you want to look through, I won't notice. Thinking of ditching all the files anyway."

Grant didn't refuse the opportunity, and he looked at each file for the period of time during which the Rymans disappeared. For each cabin, Taylor pointed to a spot on the map he had on the wall of his office, and confirmed if it was still being rented out or not. Places Taylor no longer managed, he put in a separate pile.

He had put four folders into his pack, amongst several sketchbooks and art supplies, and Taylor had returned the box to his storage room and both were into their second can of beer when someone knocked on the door.

Taylor pushed himself up and muttered, "Who's knocking this late?"

At the door he called out, "Can't you see I'm closed?"

Grant didn't hear the reply, but Taylor opened the door, and stepped back to let someone in. Grant quickly took his feet off a low table, and got to his feet.

"I'll get going then," he suggested. "It's been great hearing about the town. If you can hold that cabin, the one just up from the road, I will come in tomorrow and fix you up."

"Sorry I couldn't help you with the one your Grandad rented. It might be one of the ones that got burnt when the fire went through

The story Grant gave out was he was a writer of mystery stories and wanting somewhere quiet to work, and also to try painting. It came about so naturally when the man, Hal Taylor, began talking about the local mystery.

"Police thought they might've hired a cabin to keep out of sight like," Taylor went on. They talked to me but it was old Conroy who had hired a cabin to a local lawyer/developer guy."

"Is that the Duncan Bray guy with an office in town?"

Taylor spat a glob of saliva off the path they were currently hiking up, which led to a second cabin they went to look at. "The arrogant Mr Conroy dealt with the money crowd. I handled the lower end rentals."

Taylor laughed. "When Conroy had to retire, the owners of the cabins had to come to me to manage their rentals. "

"Did you ever rent any to Bray?"

"Nah, couldn't stand him, and he reckoned I wasn't enough of a gentleman. Besides, I heard he had a cabin of his own for when he wanted to get away from his clients."

"Does he come here often?"

"Not up this way. He checks in at his office once a month. Don't reckon he does any new business, just lets old clients catch up to him. He's too important for us now."

"So, Bray has a cabin. Did the police check that one out?" Grant asked.

"Sure did. Conroy was right annoyed. He's got a few secrets, he has. Anyway, the police swarmed that cabin and found exactly zilch."

"Did they check any other cabins?"

"Think so. Any that got rented out. A few of the empties. Thing is, there's still private cabins, old ones. Held by families."

"Where's Bray's place? Did Conroy keep it looked after when he wasn't using it?"

"Might have. I can check Conroy's old records. He gave them to me but I haven't looked at them for years. I can't take you there. Mr Bray is big on it being Private property."

Grant got the innuendo from how Taylor spoke. "Maybe I should know where it is so if I go hiking I stay right away from it," Grant suggested.

lowing the tablets, and then put the glass back on the bedside table.

Kim kissed Imogen on the cheek. "You get some rest, and take care of yourself. I want you around for a long time yet."

Imogen smiled and patted Kim's hand. "Come again soon."

"I will." Kim turned to go, holding four tablets in her hand. Until she shoved her hand in a pocket, then put the photo back in her bag. The nurse did check to see the tablets were gone, then asked Imogen if she wanted to lie down. Amherst waited for Kim to precede him out and noticed the nurse was also checking the tablets weren't hidden nearby or in the bed.

"You're not immortal, Sis. Playing with people's medication is dangerous," Adam told Kim when they were both watching TV.

"That policeman heard me say it to Imogen, and yeah, he said the same. When he realised I had palmed them and made it look like I was a concerned relative, he just produced a plastic bag and held it out. He didn't say anything then."

"Why though?"

"She said they made her forget and made her sleep. She didn't want to forget me. And I don't want her to forget me."

"You can't hide the next dose," Adam pointed out.

"I know, but she is a lonely old lady. No one ever visits her except people wanting her to sell her house or lawyers that have their own agendas. Anyway, when we left, they had the medicine trolley outside her room. Amherst took a photo of the page with her meds. They had just added a new one that morning."

"I still think it was a stupid thing to do."

"Okay, maybe it was," Kim admitted. "Have you heard from Grant?"

"Not yet. We will have to hope that Grant Fielding mystery solver is living up to his own legend."

Grant was humming to himself in satisfaction. He had been directed to the Twin Falls Hiking shop when he had asked about cabins for rent. He had specified out of the way, and unlikely to get through traffic going past. The guy behind the counter was past retirement age by his estimation, but on the plus side, he liked to talk.

suddenly blurted, "That horrible man. Came here and told me they had to be dead. He wanted me to have Elena declared dead. I told him I wouldn't believe Elena was dead unless I saw her body."

"Bray?" Kim asked.

"Duncan Bray." Imogen actually spat out the name. "He might have been Marcus's friend, but I didn't like him, even when everyone else worshipped the ground he stood on. I could tell you a few things about him."

"I don't like him either," Kim admitted. "He tried to tell my step-dad I was some kind of criminal. What did he do to you?"

The story was garbled in places but had enough detail to intrigue Amherst.

A nurse came in with medication for Imogen. "Put that on the table!" Imogen directed. "They make me sleepy and I am enjoying speaking to my granddaughter. I will take them when they leave."

"I will be back to ensure you do," the nurse warned. Imogen just waved a bony hand at her.

"I should go," Kim suggested.

"The tablets make me forget everything. I don't want to forget you. I don't want then to tell me you were a delusion. Most times, I don't care. I have nothing to do. No one visits. You will come back, won't you?"

"Every chance I can," Kim promised, then leant and whispered, "If you don't want to forget, don't take the tablets."

"Kim," Amherst warned. "They will check and it might be a bad idea to miss doses."

Kim looked at the generic white tablets, and took a photo with her phone. "Gran, would you do something for me?"

"What is it, dear child?"

"I want to be perfectly sure I am Elena's child. Would you let us take a DNA sample?"

She had to explain how easy it was and get the swab kit from Amherst. Instead of rejecting the idea, Imogen seemed suddenly animated. The process was over quickly, and the Amherst had the sample in its plastic container in his pocket when the nurse returned.

When she did, she saw Kim taking the empty medicine cup, and handing over a glass of water. Imogen took a gulp, like she was swal-

Chapter 25: A New Relative

Kim had no idea what to expect as she trailed into the care home behind her step-father and the policeman. She tried to stay unnoticed. Amherst was directed to the room occupied by Imogen Kingsley, and Kim followed obediently, but wondered why her step-father remained talking to the reception staff.

With nothing to compare the place to, Kim thought it pleasant. It smelt of fresh air and was open and tidy. The passage to the private rooms was narrower, but had various equipment stored in alcoves along one wall.

Amherst spoke to a staff member at a staff station near Imogen's room. A nurse escorted them in to speak to the elderly looking woman.

"Imogen dear, you have a visitor...no, two visitors."

The woman, sitting in a chair next to the freshly made bed, held onto a rug that was around her shoulders and turned to her visitors. She began a tirade about lawyers and real estate people who keep pestering her. Amherst, raised to be polite hadn't had a chance to speak. He gestured for Kim to approach the woman.

"Why are you here? You are too young to be a nurse."

"I'm called Kim, but my proper name is Kathryn. I think I am your granddaughter." Kim knelt beside the chair and showed her the picture of Marcus and Elena. "Did you know about me?"

Tears formed in the old woman's eyes. "Of course I knew. It was a secret, but Elena was so happy. You...look just like I remember her. Is Elena alive?"

"No one has seen her for a very long time," Kim said. "I have lived with a friend of my old nurse," Kim told her. "I only just found out about my parents."

"People keep insisting I had no grandchild. They didn't know. Claimed I was a crazy old woman."

"You are not that old!" Kim protested.

Amherst kept back, and listened to the natural way Kim brought out reminiscences. He had discreetly turned on his phone to record all they spoke of, as he watched the two women, one young, one old, forming a bond. His ears pricked up when the old woman

"We did look closely at that," Amherst remarked.

When neither Adam nor Kim had any more questions, Amherst changed topics. "You wanted to visit Imogen Kingsley?"

Kim again focused her attention on the policeman. "Do you think it's a good idea?"

"I do. I spoke to the care home. I didn't mention you but I have arranged to visit her. However, I was told she is in a fragile state and may not be either coherent or even realis we are there."

"Is she really old?" Kim asked.

"Not by normal standards. She would be in her mid-sixties."

"Then what is wrong with her?"

"I was told, early onset dementia."

"So she might not even remember she has a grandchild, or even know Elena had a child."

"It is possible. Are you alright with that?"

Kim nodded. Determined. "Yes. Has she been like that for long?"

"It came on sometime after Elena disappeared."

"Oh, that's sad," Kim said.

Jeremiah spoke then. "When should we meet you at the care home?"

The time and location of the home was related, and Amherst rose to leave. He thanked Adam and Kim for being so frank. Jeremiah saw him to the door, and Adam went back to finish the dishes. Kim started to go back to her room, but paused to listen to her step-father and the policeman talking.

"Yes, as you said, it is a good reason to take a new look at the case. That conversation between Bray and your daughter shows a different side to him. I am rather surprised he even gave her that much time. Though I am still in two minds about her being able to recall events from a decade ago, when she was a child at the time."

"I was sceptical too, but I do not wish to spurn a blessing. Until the long weekend, my daughter explained her mind had seemed cloudy. Since then, it is not only myself who has noticed the change, and her new and unusual acuity of memory. Perhaps you can compare her recall to things in the original investigation at the house."

Kim decided she had heard enough and quietly returned to her room.

finished, Amherst knew most of what they had discovered. Adam still wondered why Kim was holding back about the journal. He would ask her later.

"So, did ant of that help?" Adam asked.

"It has given me some ideas to go back over," Amherst told him. "Perhaps a visit to Eugene Bennett is an idea."

"Can you share anything about the investigation into the disappearance of Marcus and Elena?" Kim asked, looking hopeful.

"It's still an open case."

"So, no! Did Bray tell you about the cabin he told them to go to?"

"He did. There was no sign that anyone had been there."

"He's the one that had them declared dead, wasn't he?" Kim persisted.

"Yes. He was also the executor named in the will. "

"Marcus's?" Kim saw the policeman nod. "What about Elena's?"

"No, but her estate was fairly simple. All her assets went to her husband."

"Do you think that's odd, now that you have seen the birth certificate?" Adam asked.

"I do. I plan to look into that. I would have expected them to update the will when they became parents. Though sometimes intent and action are two different things."

"There was something I wondered about," Adam said. "In cases where a couple go missing or die at the same time, how do they figure out the wills?"

"Once seven years have passed, a missing person can be declared dead. When a couple do, the elder of the pair is deemed to have died first. So, the younger inherits the estate, and that and the younger one's estate go to those nominated her heirs."

"So, Elena should have inherited Marcus's estate, "Kim said, looking thoughtful.

"Usually. However, we did trace transactions from Elena's accounts – groceries, clothes, and the like for several months. Then they stopped, with money still in the account. Marcus's accounts were active after that. First for the same sort of things, nut also rent, medical expenses. They stopped abruptly a few months later."

"Someone could have used his bank cards to lay a false trail," Adam suggested.

A nod from Jeremiah had her relating their day and her reasons for going. She didn't tone down her resentment at how he told her dad she was trying to scam him.

"You recorded the conversation, I believe?"

Kim nodded, but she was chewing he lip as she did. "Was that illegal?"

"A grey area, but it was personal business and a way to recall the conversation. Will you allow me to listen to it?"

Kim had also collected her phone, so she played the conversation again. Adam noted the policeman had set his own phone to record. Amherst listened intently.

Kim murmured, "I tweaked my age up." She got a nod to indicate Amherst had heard.

"Interesting," he remarked when the recording finished. He didn't stop his phone recording when he went on. "I can attest that few people knew of you. What do you understand of what he said?"

"If he didn't know of me, he certainly didn't want to confirm I was who I claimed," Kim said defiantly. "I admit, that when I copied the birth certificate the corner was cut off. Surely though, he could look up and find it."

"Likely he could have found a way. This certainly looks legitimate. And I do have a way to check. What else can you add?"

"Adam? Mum? Can you remember what I used to say about my dreams?"

Janice nodded. Adam spoke up and described the ones a younger Kim had mentioned more than once.

"They were exactly like what I saw at the house," Kim said. "When we were there, a thunderstorm went over. Thunder has always petrified me. But this time it stimulated other memories."

Carefully, for she was not sure she would be believed, because most people could not recall things from when they were just three years old, she began to relate the new visions. "I know things like dreams can be metaphoric but I could mostly sequence the events I saw. Plus, Mr Bennett told me some things."

"Eugene Bennett?" Amherst's lips tightened.

"Yes."

"Go on."

Kim did, with Adam adding occasional comments. When they

"I'm Kim. How come you are here?" was his sister's reply.

"It's a casual chat. Why don't you sit down?"

Kim moved to the chair Adam had vacated. Adam settled onto one of the wide arms, until a glare from his step-father changed his mind. Rather than sit beside his step-father, he chose to lean against the wall, next to the unlit gas heater.

Amherst sat again before saying, "I was very surprised to have a call today from Mr Laurensen here, suggesting his children might have a new take on a thirteen year old mystery."

"Marcus and Elena Ryman," Kim told him. "I believe they are my biological parents."

"And you have proof?"

Kim hopped up. "Give me a minute, I need to get something from my room." She trotted out.

Amherst directed a question to Adam. "How did this discovery come about?"

Adam related how they had found the old house, and how Kim had recognised places in there from her dreams. At that point, Kim returned. He saw she had the photo and went on, "In the house, Mr Bennett gave us free reign. We found a child's bedroom. It look like it had been used, but the bedside drawers contained a heap of cheap toys and other junk."

Kim held up the photo. "I found this, there."

Amherst held out his hand for the picture. He glanced from Kim to the people in the photo.

"And Aunt Grace had this." Kim handed over the original of the birth certificate. That was the cue for Janice Laurensen to speak out.

Kim went back to the chair as Amherst quizzed her mum and made notes. Adam noticed she hadn't mentioned the journal yet. So she wasn't quite convinced yet to trust the visitor.

"Now, Kim. Is it alright for me to call you that, or would you prefer Kathryn?"

"Kim."

"Kim, then. I believe you spoke to Duncan Bray."

"Didn't my dad tell you?"

"Only that. He thought I should hear about it from you directly."

otherwise, Kim and I still feel the same, but we don't talk about it. Kim now seems to understand why."

"Look, I will do like I said, sound things out. I will let you know what I find."

"Thanks. Grant. I will let Kim know."

Adam was in the kitchen, taking his turn washing the dishes, when he heard the door chime. He glanced at the clock. Eight thirty at night was late for a caller. He ignored it. His step-father could tell whoever it was not a polite time to call.

He wasn't particularly eavesdropping, but was surprised that the caller had been invited in. Then alarmed when his step-father came into the kitchen.

"Leave that. Go tell your sister to come down. I want you as well."

Kim called out, "Come in," but Adam only opened the door. His sister was on the bed, a rug wrapped around her, apparently reading. She put the book aside.

"You have been summoned," Adam told her. "He's got a guest."

"Who?"

"I don't know but he wants me too."

Kim through the blanket aside, and Adam had a glimpse of a skimpy top and short shorts, as he hurriedly closed the door. It looked like she had already changed for bed. Drat her! She could have told him to 'get out' before deciding to dress decently. He didn't need his own body to betray him just now. He thought Kim understood that now.

Adam had already met the late evening guest and was distinctly uncomfortable under the eye of the senior detective. One who looked like he should have retired years ago. All he could do was sit in the chair and wait for Kim to appear. His mother sat on the couch next to his step-father, and DI Amherst had the other chair.

Kim's arrival caused the others to focus their attention on her. Adam simply stood up so Kim could have the chair. For a moment, he thought she had frozen up, like she used to with strangers, but then she took a breath and relaxed as Amherst stood up and introduced himself again.

Chapter 24: The Police Get Involved

A quiet buzz caused Adam to roll over and take his phone from beside his bed. He had deliberately turned the ring off, because he wasn't sure if phone use was included in the current 'grounding'. He had already discovered the internet didn't work.

"Hi, Grant," he said when he answered the call.

"You don't sound enthusiastic. Are you ok?"

"If you consider one's sister getting you grounded, as fine, then I am fine."

"Could be worse."

"I know, but I have come to believe Kim had bewitched him. He invited us to confess our sins and Kim asked his straight out if Bray called him to check up on her. He had, and tried to imply Kim was trying to run a scam."

"I wonder if he checked up on the old goat, too. Heard how strict he is."

"I didn't consider that. I was too busy waiting for the axe to fall. He was annoyed that Kim had gone to talk to him. I don't think he really believed what he was being told by Bray. He totally didn't when he heard what Kim had recorded. He was a bit narky she had recorded it without asking Bray if she could, but he accepted it as being a way for her to recall things that might help her find her parents."

"I was going to ask if you wanted to drive back to Twin Falls with me to try to find out about the cabin Bray mentioned."

"Sorry, mate. It turns out I am not free for the next week. There's nothing stopping you...and you could take Paula."

"About that, and don't get me wrong, I'd love to. It's just ... things your step-father told you, kind of hit a nerve. Paula and I have been friends for years, but I never realised people could be petty about things now I am eighteen and she'd not."

"At least she isn't believed to be your sister," Adam said quietly.

"So that's what set the old goat off,' Grant only commented, referring back to the long weekend. "Have things changed now we know Kim was adopted?"

"I doubt it," Adam decided. We still use the same name, but

"My girl, you continue to surprise me with your innate compassion. And maybe I should not be disappointed you are not perfect. You should have come to me and talked of this. However I can understand why you may not have felt comfortable doing so. Will you trust me to look into ways for you to meet your grandmother? What can you tell me?"

Kim really only knew her name, but Jeremiah accepted that.

Then Kim surprised him once again, by throwing herself at him to give him a hug. "Thank you."

This time though, his expression softened.

"Then you will also understand that I gave my word that I would 'control' my daughter. So for the next week, you will not leave this house. Nor will your brother. For I am still certain you would not have considered visiting a total stranger without his support."

Kim released him and stepped back, looking down. "Yes, I understand."

When Jeremiah queried Adam he muttered, "Yes, Sir."

"I'm sorry, Adam," Kim muttered, just audibly.

"Yeah, well, I wasn't going to let you go alone. You'd have probably got yourself lost."

"It is well you both are growing in maturity," Jeremiah commended. "Now I suggest you each spend some time in private meditation. Go."

Adam followed Kim upstairs. At the top, he muttered, "I swear you have bewitched him. Hugging him? When he turns around and grounds us?"

"You complaining about that?"

"No," Adam growled. "We really didn't do anything wrong." And, he thought privately, he'd take grounding any day in lieu of another beating.

"Did I need to? I just wanted a way to remember all he told me, in case there were other ways I could confirm who I was, and find out what happened to my birth parents."

"Very well, play the recording."

Kim found the file on her phone and replayed it on the speaker.

While the severe expression didn't change, the tension in her step-father did.

"What Bray had to say, I did not want to believe. When he told me I needed to control my daughter better, before she was arrested for trying to perpetuate a fraud, I was astounded."

"What did you say to him?" Kim dared to ask.

"I told him you were normally too shy to speak to strangers, so your reason to visit him had to be important. I did promise I would speak to you."

Kim held her breath.

"My opinion of Bray after hearing your recording, is not favourable. Having said that, I do not think it wise for you to speak with him again."

"I didn't like him either," Kim admitted. "And truly, I never even considered I was potentially able to claim money somehow. I still don't understand if it is possible."

"So why did you still want confirmation after my wife's good word and the birth certificate?"

Kim wrung her hands without realising what she was doing, betraying her indecision.

"I did feel that proved it to me. That and seeing the things in the house, and the picture of the people I saw in my dreams. But I still want to know what happened to them. I thought their good friend, Bray might have known something he never told the police."

"Is that all?"

"No..."

"Go on."

"If they are my parents – Marcus and Elena – no one knew about me. Elena's mum is still alive, in a care home. Surely she deserves to know about me. But...I can't just go see her, with a birth certificate. I could have got that anywhere. If Bray is trying to make out I am a criminal, deny my existence, no one will let me meet her."

old mattresses for the girls."

"Where is this all going? Particularly since you both knew I told you to keep away from each other."

"It was my doing," Kim admitted. "But it is relevant to what you asked." Then, in as few words as possible, she told him how she had matched her old recurring dreams to places in the house. "And the guy said I was the image of someone he once knew that had lived in that house. That person and her husband vanished a dozen or so years ago."

Adam's mother, Janice took over. "They turned up at my sister's place while I was there. Kim told us how her dreams were real, when I had always told her they were just dreams. I felt it best to tell her the truth then. Kim is not my biological daughter. My sister worked as a nanny for Marcus and Elena Ryman. One night, they had to leave. Someone was after them. They told my sister to get their daughter away and keep her safe. She came to me. I had just lost my second child and a husband I had loved, but we both agreed the child would be safer with me. Grace had Kim's birth certificate and gave it to her."

Jeremiah's expression indicated a degree of disappointment in his wife, even if it was only having withheld that detail.

"Jeremiah, when I met you a few years later, Kim was my daughter. Her parents had not returned, and they still haven't."

Kim was told to continue, and she paused to sort through what she knew. To tell just enough to justify her reason to go and see Bray.

"So, I wasn't trying to scam anyone. I had no idea I had been adopted until I saw the house and recognised the places there. It made sense, but Mum had never said anything. I was just looking for confirmation."

"I was told that Marcus Ryman was very wealthy and had no heirs," Jeremiah stated.

"Yes, he told me that. But I had a birth certificate."

"Which he can't confirm."

"I don't know how he could think I was trying to scam him," Kim said directly. "I recorded the conversation, you can listen and see what you think."

"Did you get permission to record it?"

Chapter 23: Trouble at Home

While Gavin drove them home from the station, Adam rang his mum. She was put shopping but promised to be home soon as she could. Had gone silent, dreading the confrontation to come. One relieving sight was seeing her mum's car in the drive when they got home.

Instead of waiting for the inevitable summons, Kim went directly to find her step-father. That he was pacing the lounge room, was not a good sign.

"What did you want to see me about?" Kim asked.

Jerimiah Laurensen turned, and Kim felt like she was a rodent he had just spotted.

"Is there something you should be telling me?"

That was promising, even if his expression was just short of angry.

Kim made a quick decision and went on the defensive. "Mr Bray called to check on me?" she asked, meeting his gaze.

"Yes, indeed. Exactly what kind of scam were you trying to pull?"

"I was not doing anything like that," Kim told him without looking away. "I went to see him to verify some information and to ask some questions."

"Perhaps you would be kind enough to explain?" He gestured for her to sit down, and took another chair for himself.

"On the long weekend, I knew Grant and Adam intended to go to hike around Golden Falls. I convinced Paula to come with me to meet them. I wanted to see the falls. I had heard about the place. I found out the falls weren't all that great, and we were returning to town by a different trail and came across an old abandoned house. Grant and Adam had tents and stuff since they had intended to camp out, but before we found a spot, the storm broke. I...lost it."

Adam took over. "We went back to the house and knocked in case someone was there. NO one answered, so we set up the tents under some trees back from it. It turned out that a guy was staying there. He got back late. By then, the tent Grant and I were using had collapsed. In any case, the guy offered us room inside where we could put out the hiking rolls and we helped him bring down two birth certificate and maybe what was at the house, not all the other stuff...”

"We will need to tell mum to tell him it's true," Adam decided.

"We can play that recording so he knows exactly what I said," Kim added. "And cross our fingers."

None of them had an answer to that.

"If we are finished, why don't we take a tram down to the beach?" Paula suggested.

"Good idea," Grant agreed. "We can give our minds a rest."

As they sat on the sand, Grant said, "We are probably right about Bray having a will of Marcus's, though it may not be the latest will. He'd have all his personal information anyway, but would he have had Elena's will?"

Shrugs all round.

"Do you think he would keep those records in his office?" Kim asked.

"In his big fancy law firm office?" Grant considered. "I don't reckon so. I mean, he's been in the firm for over ten years. Any stuff from Marcus was before that. He probably dealt with all that at his office in Twin Falls. If he kept the files, that's where I think they would be."

"Which means, we can't see them," Adam stated flatly.

"What if I say I have more questions and ask to meet him there?" Kim proposed.

"Let's keep that idea in reserve," Adam suggested.

"Yeah," Paula agreed.

Adan's phone rang. "Hello, yes, Kim's with me. Yes, okay, we'll be home in an hour."

"What?" Kim asked.

"He wants us home," Adam told her. "I have a horrid feeling that Bray checked up on you and found our address, and rang to mention your visit."

Kim felt like her gut dropped ten feet.

"We are going to have to tell him," Adam warned her.

"He's trying to scare us off," Kim responded.

"Bray?" Grant guessed. "He's probably just beginning. However, in the scheme of things, we have done nothing illegal."

"Illegal, no. Just lied by omission," Adam muttered. He saw Grant's sympathetic grin.

"He listened to us about those bullies at school," Kim reminded Adam. "If we admit everything, well about the photo and

He'd had three years to do it."

"Perhaps he did," Adam agreed. "He may not have done it through Bray."

"He applied to have them declared dead after five or so years," Paula reminded them. "What rationale did he have when he'd convinced them they were in mortal peril if they stayed around? Do you know?"

"I am sure all reasonable enquiries were made. I would assume they would have had notices in the papers," Grant guessed.

"Do you think Bray will get back in touch with me?" Kim asked.

"If he bought your 'simple' persona, he will get back with official sounding proof that even if you are Ryman's kid, there is nothing for you."

"So what do we do now?" Kim asked.

"I'd say, wait to see if he does get back to you," Adam voiced his opinion.

"And while we wait, go over what you recorded while you were there, and compare it to what we know. It sounds like he stuck fairly close to the truth, but like you said, if his time line was out..."

"Short of asking him, I wonder if there is a way to find out about that rental cabin," Paula suggested.

"Maybe," Grant considered. "Might be a longshot."

"You know," Adam spoke after a period of silence. "We know Bray saw to having them declared dead, Might he have a record of his reasons, apart from them not being seen?"

"You might not need more than that," Grant guessed. "I can look that up when I get home, and check if I can find out how hard he did try to find them."

"I am sure they wouldn't have just abandoned me," Kim said. "But Bray didn't know about me then. He went and saw Aunt Grace, who he thought was the housekeeper. We should ask her more about that. What else was I going to say....oh, yes! He put a will in for probate, and must have had access to Marcus's financial details to know there was money missing. Could that have implied he was still alive somewhere?"

"None of us have legal knowledge," Adam pointed out. "We can only guess. Bray is a top lawyer. He'd know all the ins and outs."

Looking like she was loathe to part with the photo. She let Bray look at it. His expression as he looked from the photo to her, didn't change, but a tic started in his right cheek.

"That is a truly remarkable resemblance," he admitted. His expression softened, but the tic remained. He sat back and seemed to be thinking.

"You are 18?" Bray prompted.

"Eighteen and a half," Kim claimed. That made her two years older than she was.

"Maybe that explains why they married in a hurry."

"Excuse me?" Kim asked.

"Marcus and Elena," Bray explained in a quiet, matter of fact tone. "They kept it secret. The asked me to be a witness. Then they went off on a long honeymoon. Marcus got in touch with me when he returned, but never mentioned a child. I would have expected him to have updated his will to include his child, if he had one. I can only assume, if there was a child, you weren't his. That Elena had already been pregnant."

Kim shoved a fist in her mouth, then said, "But...but...his name is on the certificate."

Bray waved that consideration aside. "No doubt it was to preserve his, and Elena's reputation."

"But where are they now?" Kim asked like a lost soul.

"I am sorry to be unable to help you," Bray sounded sincere, "but I can only assume they are dead. However, no one has found any trace of them. I know the police suspected someone, an ex-boyfriend of Elena's. He made a scene soon after they returned. It was ugly. I advised them to stay elsewhere until the matter was resolved, but they wouldn't. After that I heard rumours about someone being after them. The young fool wouldn't listen until it was almost too late. Someone told me about an intended visit to the old house. I went there to warn them, but I was too late."

"They were dead?"

"No, gone. There was a thug on the floor, knocked out. I called the police, but reception was poor at the house. I was on my way to report to the police, when Marcus called me. He sounded like he was in a panic. He didn't know where to go to be safe. I gave him the address of a cabin I rented sometimes. I said I would call them

"How can I help you, Miss Laurensen?" Duncan Bray wore a conservative suit, a collared shirt and a tie that somehow screamed, 'Wealthy. Successful'. His dark hair was starting to go grey at the temples.

He gestured to a chair in front of his desk and walked around to the executive chair behind it.

"Um...I hope you can help me. You see, I just turned 18, and about a week later, I received a letter. I don't know who sent it, but ...it was addressed to me, but had a birth certificate for someone called, Kathryn Imogen Marie Ryman. That said my parents were Marcus and Elena Ryman."

Kim looked right at Bray and saw the shift in his gaze from casual and superior, to intent.

"It had a deed to a property, a copy I think, at a place called Twin Falls. I went there. To the house, but some guy said he'd bought it. So I went back to town. A woman I spoke to said you were the local solicitor, years back. I hoped you might know something. I tried your office there, but it wasn't open. I had to do an internet search to find you."

"Marcus Ryman was the son of a very good friend of mine," Bray admitted. "He became like a son when his father died."

Kim stared intently, hanging on every word. "You did know them! What happened to them?"

"You mentioned a birth certificate," Bray prompted.

Kim rifled through the shoulder bag she had with her, and took out a folded sheet of paper. It conveniently had part of the registration number torn off when the copy was made.

"Do you also have the land title?"

Kim nodded. That was something Grant's mate had obtained. It was old, but authentic.

Bray studied it, or seemed to be. Kim thought he was studying her over the top of it.

"I don't know who is trying to cause trouble, Miss Laurensen, but to my knowledge, Marcus and Elena Ryman had no children."

Kim took out the photo of her real parents. "I...didn't know I was adopted until I received the letter. I couldn't ask my parents, they are both gone now, but my aunt said my mum had this photo and I look just like her."

"Have you lived up here since then?" Adam asked.

"No. This place belongs to a mate. He let me come here a couple of years ago. But before that, I was living off the grid. Drunk most of the time. I blamed myself for Elena and Marcus disappearing. As time went on, I figured they had to be dead. And if they were, and were found, I'd be the one they come after. But it wasn't me."

"I believe you," Kim said gently, squeezing his hand.

Grant came to squat near Bennett. "Apart from passion, another reason people get hurt his money. They were both rich, weren't they?"

"I didn't know who Marcus was when I first saw him, but I learned about him from the papers. He inherited the family you know why that fortune. Elena though, her family was wealthy too but her mother was still alive, and she had the money."

"Is she still alive?" Paula thought to ask.

"Haven't tried to find out. I'm the last person she'd want to see." Bennett said, morosely. "I don't care about the money."

Grant waited a moment. "Why do you think people might have been after him, forgetting about his fortune for a moment?"

"What little I heard in the pub that day, didn't tell me much. I just got the idea some powerful person wanted to know where he was. Something about poking in where he shouldn't."

"Do you know Duncan Bray?" Grant asked.

Bennett looked confused "You can't think he's involved?"

"No, just trying to find out if he knew Marcus or Elena. He might throw some light on things," Grant suggested.

"Back then... he probably moved in the same circles as Marcus," Bennet suggested. "He didn't like me, not surprising. I thought for a while he was wanting a chance to her himself. Elaine said, "Don't be silly. He's my cousin."

Grant glanced at Adam, a tacit, "any questions?"

"Can you think of anything that might help us find where Marcus and Elena went?" Kim asked. "I know it's been a while, but over time you might have thought of something."

"If I could, I'd tell you. For your own sake, and for Elena's, maybe

Waited. Finally, I tried the handle and it opened. The house was eerily quiet. Everything looked normal but it was like all the hairs on my neck wanted to stand up. I went into the lounge and saw the picture of Elena. I wanted to keep it, but I put it back. At that point, I called out and when no one answered, I tip-toed upstairs. In the master bedroom, the wardrobe doors were open, but lots of clothes were still there. All the other rooms were empty. I realised though that Elena and Marcus must have already been married, and at that, I just had to get out."

people had been asking about Marcus and Elena. And, word they come to the dance had already got around. Long and short of it, I sucked it up that she didn't want me, knew it was for the best... I did have a temper... I had been in trouble with the police at the time or two and she deserved better. So I wanted to apologise, but I also wanted to warn them."

"So, what happened?"

"I... I didn't do it right. I felt I had to try once more to get her back. Marcus, he didn't give me a chance to apologise ... Oh, it all went wrong. I ended up saying 'the hell with you' and leaving. I didn't even mention my fears about people asking about them."

"You may have gone about it wrong," Kim told him. "But after that, he decided I needed to go to somewhere else. Maybe he already knew he was in danger - but however it was, I got away and no one knew about me."

"Yes, but don't you see, that's exactly why you don't need to get involved now," Bennett pleaded. "You're all that's left of her!"

"Surely what happened a decade ago no longer matters," Adam suggested.

"Some people have been long memories and too much to hide," Bennett said obliquely.

"Who do you mean?" Grant asked.

"I should have tried harder," Bennett went on, as if not hearing the question. "And I should have just walked away! But I really did love Elena."

"The paper said the police picked you up," Kim said.

"They did that. I don't blame them for thinking I'd done something to them. When people realised they were missing, they went to the house. The place had been ransacked, but there had been two half-drunk drinks on the kitchen bench and the lights had been left on. They said I'd done it in a rage, and they found my prints on the doorknob and a picture of Elena. Tried to get me to say what I'd done, to tell them where they were, but I didn't know. The whole town looked at me like I was guilty. Elaine was liked by everyone. No one was happy I had been released."

"How did your prints get on those things," Grant asked.

"Oh, that. I did go back again. The lights were on. I just intended to stay at the door, apologise and go. I'm knocked and got no answer.

"I didn't, truly. What I did know was that I'd always dreamed of certain things and didn't know why. Now I do."

"Better you forget again."

"I guess you know how hard it is, but I needed to know." Kim insisted. "I don't think you did anything to Elena, or to Marcus. I heard you'd argued with her at the dance, and came to the house to talk to her again. You threw a vase, you didn't kill anyone."

"How... did you know that? Bennett stared at her now.

"I was three. I sneaked out, because of the storm, but the angry voice's scared me. I saw you. And yes, in every bad dream I've had, I saw you. Yet, I knew you had gone."

Kim tried to interpret Bennett's expression. It was like she was some kind of lifeline.

"You left. Marcus and Elena had already decided that I had to go to stay somewhere else. My nurse was already packing. Elena was stripping the bed. I was being carried down an old stairway when someone started pounding on the door."

"Who?"

"I don't know. I didn't see who it was. I found out yesterday that, as my nurse was driving away, Marcus's car passed her, going fast."

Bennett moved his hand so it now covered hers. He didn't speak right away, but Kim didn't try to hurry him. She thought, maybe, he had even more bad memories of that time.

"You are right, I was angry that night. Seeing Elena at the dance, obviously smitten with Marcus... I saw red. I just got discharged from the army. I came back for her. I thought we had an understanding before I left. Of course, I was kicked out from the dance, so I drove off, drove around. I stopped for a drink at a rather shady bar. It was a regular place for me. I overheard some talk that at first didn't mean much. Then an old acquaintance found me. Asked about me and Elena and did I know she was engaged?"

"I said, I'd found she was as good as. Then the guy said I'd be better off keeping away from her. I just agreed, slammed down the mug and stalked out."

"So, why did you go and see her again that night?" Kim asked.

"Something I'd heard said, suddenly made sense. Mac, the guy who came over, was an old friend. I realised he was looking out for me and obliquely warning me. What I realised though, was that

Chapter 16: Confronting a Suspect

Kim knocked on the wooden door of a secluded wood cabin. Grant had already noticed security cameras using the small pair of binoculars he had with him.

"I don't think he welcomes to visitors," Grant had warned. But Kim was determined, so he, Adam and Paula stood behind her.

When no one came to answer the knock, Adam strolled to the side to look around. He returned to say, "There's a car parked behind the shack."

Kim knocked again. "We know you're in there, Mr Bennett. We just want to talk to you."

After a minute, they heard the sound of bolts being drawn back. The door opened slowly, Bennett glanced passed his visitors and mumbled, "You might as well come in, then." He stepped aside, and closed the door after them. He shuffled forward to chuck a newspaper off one chair, a pile of just washed clothes off another. He removed several empty beer cans from a low table.

"There's nothing more to say,
" Bennett told them. "I don't know what happened to them."

Kim noticed he was looking at everyone but her. She took a breath and said, "Why did you run off?"

He looked at her and it was like he wanted to flee again. His hand reached for a full can of beer, sitting open on the mantle over the fireplace. Then he snatched it back.

Adam suggested, "Why don't you sit down, Mr Bennett?" His voice was gentle and Bennett seemed to slump and stumbled the two steps to the nearest chair.

"Why did you have to come?" he accused them. "Why did you have to stir things up again?"

Kim came and perched on the low table then reached out to place her hand on his.

"I'm sorry I remind you so much of Elena."

"You shouldn't have gone there."

"I didn't know what was there," Kim told him. "I didn't know anything about those who lived there."

"But…"

"He might be, but those he talks to might have reason to pass that information on."

"No. You have a point. Maybe he'll just see what he can find out about Marcus and Elena. He might uncover something new."

Kim agreed to that much and Grant said he'd get onto that after they'd seen Bennett. Then asked, "You still sure you want to confront him?"

"Confront, no. I just want to ask him about Marcus and Elena."

"Okay, we will get moving on."

The reply, "What?"

Kim sent, "Over breakfast?"

Adam sent, "Okay," with a frown emoji.

Grant announced that he'd tracked down Bennett's current address, and could they wait for breakfast until they were down the road a bit.

"How did you find him?" Paula asked.

"Grant Fletcher, mystery solver has his ways!"

"No, really?" Paula encouraged.

"I have a friend, Murph, who does background checks for businesses aiming to hire people. I owe him a six-pack."

With several bags of food, sandwiches and pies, and drinks, Grant drove from the small town, to a spot on the river upstream from the dam. They were alone, except for the birds flitting from tree to tree.

Once everyone had eaten, Grant said, "so what do you have Kim?"

Kim had the book in her jacket pocket, and now produced it so the boys could look through it. Adam read the end pages first, speaking aloud for Grant's benefit. Then he passed it over and Grant looked at the pages of cryptic entries.

"Well?" Kim prompted.

"Some numbers might be bank account details," Grant murmured. "Some might be dates. Initials to indicate people. Would you let me take a shot of each page?"

"So long as no one can access it on your phone," Adam added. Kim nodded.

"It sounds important," Paula commented. "So why was it put in a kid's diary, and left in an unlocked drawer."

Kim was quiet, then said, "Someone came to the house, Banged on the door. Marcus told Elena they had to leave - right away. Maybe Marcus didn't have time to put it in his safe, if he had one. And didn't want it on him. Probably no one would think to look in a kid's diary, hidden amongst cheap kid's toys in a room that looked like no kids lived there."

"You thinking of getting Murph to look at it?" Adam asked. "Do we really want other people aware we have that data?"

"Murphy's discreet," Grant assured him.

Kim didn't argue and pushed the book back into the glittery cover and then into her pack. She was more than ready to have her turn in the shower.

Once in bed, she relaxed into the comfortable mattress and expected to be asleep in no time. After a long time with her eyes shut, breathing evenly, she was still awake. She tried to think of the bedroom, the image hadn't come. Rolling over onto a new position didn't help either.

"Maybe it's just being in a strange bed," she whispered to herself, realising this was the first time she had been away from home to sleep, discounting Paula's place. For something to focus on, she recalled the visions that had come to her at the house. The new ones not the old, repetitive ones. Now she knew who smiling faces belonged to and who they were. Funny, she decided, she'd not remembered Aunt Grace as her minder. Had something else happened to cause her mind to blur those memories? Even 13 years on, Kim could recall the sense of terror, knowing her parents were frightened, her nurse was frightened.

Her mind focused on the banging on the door, hearing her father saying they had to leave, right then.

"Why?" Kim asked herself. Had Bennett returned? Had he done something to them? No. He'd gone off and they'd not felt they needed to leave until later, they just wanted her to go to a safer place for a short time.

"Someone was after them," Kim realised. "Did someone else come in and throw the knife? Was it whoever banged on the door?

No way to tell. She hadn't seen who it was. Then she recalled the envelope Aunt Grace had given her and decided to look inside, see what was on her birth certificate.

It was surreal. It didn't seem real that the certificate referred to her, but what details she had matched. Her parents had only been in their twenties. Elaine had been a local girl, but Marcus had been born in the city. Not much use at the moment, but she needed it for getting it learner's permit and driver's license. Or would she? If she had been adopted, what ID could she get in the name she used now? Another question to ask in the morning.

Sleep finally came, but Kim woke early and sent Adam a text. "Something to show you."

Chapter 15: The Hidden Journal

Kim and Paula, both wishing they didn't have to separate from the boys, did admit they were tired. The previous night had not been restful, and their beds far from comfortable. They both expected to sleep deeply, since no storms were likely to roll over.

While Paula had her shower, Kim went through her pack for her toiletries bag and a change of underwear. Her hand touched what felt like a book, and she remembered what she had found in the drawer in the old bedroom.

She drew it out. It was...she recalled the smiling woman giving it to her...for her birthday. Now she considered it, she'd have been too young to know how to write, she had only scribbled. Enjoying the memory, she tried to open it, but the very simple lock held it shut. Looking at the edges, she realised the paper inside wasn't the gilt edged paper she remembered. Instead of trying to open it, she pushed on the book inside, and a small but thick note book fell out. It had a plain black cover and she had never seen it before.

Curious, she opened it at the front. There was no name in the space for a name, but the writing was neat and small. The numbers and cryptic notations meant nothing to her as she flipped over one page after another. Then she found a readable paragraph. Mentions of threatening calls, the sense of being watched, and fears that someone he trusted was leaking confidential information. The very last entry read, "It has to be Bray."

"Kim!" Paula repeated when her comment about being out of the shower got no reaction.

Wordlessly, Kim handed her the book at the place where the writing made sense.

"Where'd you get this?"

"I found it in the drawer of the little bedroom. It was inside this... she showed her the glittery cover."

"We need to show this to the guys."

"It can wait until morning," Kim told her. "It's too late to think about it."

Paula yawned. "Stuff it back in your back then."

“I need to know the truth.”

“Okay, we will all go with you. That should be safe enough,” Adam agreed.

"We think, it could be a reason why Ryman..."Adam began.

"Might have been killed," Kim finished. "So Bennett's claim he didn't kill Elena might be truth."

"So, was there anything else?" Kim asked.

"Politically, about the time Marcus disappeared, there was a lot of accusations of bribery, impropriety, fraud..." Grant trailed off. "Nothing I could link to the disappearance."

"So we are nowhere still," Paula summarised.

"That's it in a nutshell," Grant admitted.

"What about Bennett?" Kim asked. "I think I believe him but where did he go? Why did he run?"

"I think," Adam said, "He was afraid we would dredge up the past, and he would be a suspect all over again."

"Surely not," Paula countered.

"We know he had a temper," Adam said. He caused a scene in public. He was questioned vey rigorously. They found his fingerprints on a picture, and the door knob, but they had no proof then, of foul play. Even though they released him, the town turned against him."

"Where did he go?" Kim asked. "Did he come back now to buy the house where Elena had been?"

"He said that," Adam reminded her.

"I know. I'm trying to figure out why he'd bother. He was opening himself up to a lot of pain. We should talk to him again awe can all go together."

"He might know more," Grant considered. "And talking to him, would be better than asking questions of random people."

"Where does he live," Paula asked.

"I think I have a line on his place," Grant revealed. "There is a land line listed under E. Bennett, and from the number sequence, it is one of the earliest lines established here. We spoke to the local librarian, the place is likely upside of that hill beyond the lake. I did a google maps search but can't see many places up there."

"Tomorrow then," Kim insisted. "What about Bray?"

"He still has an office in Twin Falls," Grant said. "I don't think he still lives around here."

"What are you thinking of doing, Kim?" Adam asked.

The picnic table wasn't near the barbecues, or any of the occupied tables.

"So, what's the news?" Paula demanded.

"Okay, Adam and I found an internet café and did some research. I did a search on Bray. Duncan Bray is well respected, involved in developing land, local politics and was a former financial advisor. I couldn't find anything adverse about him."

"He knew Marcus Ryman," Kim reminded them. "Was he just a friend?"

"We don't know," Adam told her.

"I also did a search on Adam's step-father," Grant said. That gave him everyone's full attention.

"I don't know if you realise it, but he is very important with respect to his church. He is also consulted on matters relating to health and wellbeing. He is known for advocating low cost residences for people in hard ship."

"Well, good for him," Kim muttered.

"He has a lot of powerful friends," Adam summarised.

"So, can he help find what happened to Marcus and Elena Ryman?" Kim challenged.

"I don't know, but we might need to ask his help."

"Not unless we are desperate," Kim stated.

"Fine," Adam agreed. Grant suggested it and I didn't like the idea any more than you did."

"Alright, forget that idea," Grant accepted. "Moving on, Adam and I were scrutinising the local paper. One subject was the dam."

"Which you said went ahead after Ryman was declared dead," Kim remembered.

"Yes, I tried to get the background story. All I picked up was there was a lot of controversy. Ryman owned the land where the lake is and the resort. As well as a lot of land down river. He refused to sell any of it to be developed. Those who wanted the resort were quite vocal, saying it would bring money to the town. Which it did, but what I think is that the developer is getting most of the benefit."

"So who is the developer?" Paula asked.

The company he mentioned meant nothing to them.

"I haven't been able to find anything on the people behind the company," Grant admitted.

Chapter 14: Who to Blame?

Grant and Adam were waiting at the coffee shop down the road from Twin Falls Lake Resort. They rolled their eyes at the number of bags the girls had.

"Did you leave anything for anyone else?" Grant teased. "Do you want to put the bags in my car?"

Both girls nodded. Grant told Adam, "Mind the table. We won't be long."

They weren't since Grant had found a parking spot not far from the café. Once back, they found the waitress had left menus, so they decided what they wanted. Kim and Paula had stopped for a milk shake, but they hadn't eaten.

"We've booked two small cabins for tonight," Adam told the girls. We were lucky to get them, since it's a long weekend."

How much will it cost?" Paula asked with concern.

"Grant and I split the cost. We've not been splurging all afternoon."

"What were you two doing," Kim asked.

"Looking around," Adam said. "I'll fill you in later."

At the caravan park, Grant said, "Which one do you girls want? Right or left?"

Since both of the tiny cabins were identical, Paula shrugged and said, "Left." Grant tossed her the relevant key.

"Settle in," Grant said. "Meet us in half an hour. We can walk to the lake and talk there."

"Why there?" Paula asked. Grant scuffed his foot on the gravel of a path to the cabins.

"It's out in the open. I don't want people seeing Adam and I going into your cabin, or you two coming into ours."

Paula opened her mouth to protest, but Kim said, "Are we being watched?"

"It's just that I got quizzed about our intentions," Grant said.

"What?" Paula blurted. "How did they even know about us?"

"It's okay, Paula. Grant is right," Kim told her. "You and I are still under age."

"Alright, half an hour. Will you have a groundsheet?"

"Mum is right, he does look after us."

"And he will think you suitably repentant?" Paula suggested, slyly.

"I hope so," Kim admitted. "This is something I think he will like. It's simple, handmade, useful...I hope. He's not into fancy stuff."

"Fair enough. I like that carved jewellery box," Paula admitted.

"That's for Mum. How about this box for Aunt Grace? Do you think it could hold her crochet hooks?"

"I think so. What else have you found?"

"Just a keyring," Kim said as if it was nothing special. "What's the time?"

"Three thirty. We should hear from Grant soon."

"I'll go and pay for these things," Kim said.

"We need to finish drying our stuff out," Adam reminded her.

"And I need to get back to my car," Grant added.

"You can do that. Kim and I can take the bus," Paula told him.

"Are you really okay with everything," Paula asked Kim as they walked to the bus stop.

"No. I never expected to learn what I did," Kim admitted.

""Why did you mention Golden Falls?" Paula asked, curious.

"I heard mum mention the place. She was on the phone, maybe to Aunt Grace."

"I am happy it helped you clear the brain fog."

"That, yes," Kim agreed. "It's rather like being half blind and suddenly seeing clearly. And I feel vindicated. I knew I'd had another life."

"Well, I won't be telling anyone," Paula assured her. You would not want people to think you're delusional if you claim to be an heiress."

"You are right, though that idea never occurred to me. Aunt Grace, when she mentioned Bray, and something about settling the estate, got me thinking that if no one knew about me, his fortune is probably long gone."

Paula paused before adding, "You'd be a target if whoever did inherit sees you as a threat."

"We need to talk to Eugene," Kim decided.

"I am really not sure that's a good idea," Paula cautioned.

"Fair enough," Kim seemed to agree. "Besides we don't know where he ran off to anyway."

"And why did he run off? What if it was to tell someone you exist?"

"I can't see myself as a threat to anyone," Kim admitted. "And don't worry, I don't plan to do anything stupid."

Shopping kept them busy for hours. Mostly, they bought girl things. Kim said, she thought her step-father would expect that. However, she also wanted to find special gifts for her mother, aunt and step-father.

"You don't really like him," Paula remarked as Kim fingered an artisan carved wooden dish.

deer look he knew so well. He glanced at Grant and lifted his own phone in a silent question. Had something he read online prompted the question?

"I don't think so," Grace sighed.

"No one would dare risk Jeremiah's anger," Janice declared. It was obvious she believed that.

Adam winced. He had learnt that, all too well, all too recently.

Grant got busy on his phone again but said nothing. Grace stood up and went to her bedroom.

"What do you all plan to do now," Janice asked. "Head home?"

"No," Kim stated. "Not until late tomorrow. There's stuff I need to think about."

Grace returned to the lounge with a legal sized envelope.

Adam shook his head, though his reasons were different. Are you going to tell our step-father we were all here together?" He asked his mother.

She didn't answer right away. "No. however, he will likely notice the change in Kim and wonder how it came about."

"We can't tell him," Kim pleaded. "If people remain ignorant of who I am, no one will bother us. And really the only one this matters to is me, I won't let him notice much difference."

She took the envelope from her aunt, saw the return address, and slipped the envelope in her bag.

Kim had grown up, Adam realised. The aura of child-like innocence had gone. A subtle hint of secrecy had replaced it. He doubted her feelings for him had changed, any more than his, for her. She now understood, actions had consequences.

"We could do a trip out to the lake. The girls said they were planning to do shopping," Grant suggested. "They have that rock wall climbing thing out there too."

"Is dad still mad at us," Kim asked.

"You should know my now, he gets angry, yes, and punishes you. But if you realise you were wrong, and accept it, as far as he is concerned, that is the end of it," Janice told her.

"Shopping," Paula said, breaking the uncomfortable silence. I can do that. When do we leave?"

Chapter 13: A Clearer Mind

"Jeremiah Laurensen is a good man," Janice said. "Yes, he is strict in his beliefs, but he provides well for us."

"Was that all you wanted, mum? Someone to provide for us?" Kim asked.

"No," Grace contradicted, "When we thought things had settled down, someone came to see me. He knew I had worked for Marcus for a time, as a housekeeper. He said he was needing to finalise the estate. He had applied to have Marcus declared dead. Said, since I had not been given proper notice, I was due a month's pay. He did seem to know how much I was being paid. Then he seemed interested to know if I had heard anything since that night. Which I hadn't."

"Who was it?" Adam asked.

Grace shuddered. "Bray. I remember thinking he reminded me of a braying donkey. He had that brash assurance that everything he said was true. I had heard of him, Marcus knew him, but face to face, something about him gave me the shivers."

"Can you recall his first name?" Grant asked.

"No...I don't think so."

"Duncan," Kim blurted, swiping a sleeve across her eyes before turning. "I remember hearing the name, I thought it was Uncle Bray the first few times."

"I'll see if I can find anything," Grant decided, bringing out his phone.

Adam saw the pain in Kim's eyes and wasn't sure if it was because she had discovered her biological parents and found out they were surely dead, or if it was because her deepest hopes were likely impossible to achieve.

He didn't feel any happier himself, but he had to seem impassive. The residual soreness in his back became his focus. He understood things better than Kim did, but she was coming to realise the things he had to hide.

Hearing Grant ask, "Do you think Kim is still in any danger?" sent a thrust of fear into Adam's heart. Kim took on the startled

dangerous for you to stay with Grace. That's when we decided I would look after you. I told one or two close friends I was needing to go and visit an old friend who was ill. I left Adam with Grace and a month later, returned. During that time, I sold the house I had lived in with Adam's father, and bought this one. I settled in here, and everyone thought you and Adam were both mine."

"Did you really think Kim was in that much danger?" Grant asked.

"We both did," Grace admitted. "I had started hearing things too, snippets. I was visited by the police, because the house was ransacked. I told them everything except about Kim. I started recalling parts of conversations between Marcus and Elena, but it didn't help me figure out what happened to them. I really feared the worst, but I had promised them I would keep Kathryn safe."

"Was that my name?" Kim asked.

"Your real name is Kathryn Imogen Marie Ryman. You were always called Kim. Imogen was for Elena's mother, Marie for Marcus's."

"Is there a birth certificate?" Kim asked.

"Yes, but I waited a few months before going down to the city to register it."

"Do you have a copy?"

"Yes, Marcus had one too which he out in a safe place. Not at the house."

Kim stood up and paced the room. "Do you think they are dead?"

Grace admitted, I think they must be, or they would have returned for you, long since."

"Everyone thinks Bennett did something to them," Janice spoke with more than a trace of displeasure. "But nothing could be proved,"

Kim went to stare out a window. The elation she hoped to feel, was non-existent. Apart from her old nanny, and the woman she had called her mum for years, she didn't exist. Well, she did, but as Kim Laurensen. With her step-father's name.

"Why did you marry again?" Kim asked. She had turned so no one could see there the feelings she couldn't hide. Needing to hide her feelings hadn't changed since finding out her proper name.

he had gone. She was upset, but put on a brave face for you."

Kim didn't tell the attempt had faired. She had sensed her mother's terror.

"She told me to go, and then began stripping the bed. Then someone came and pounded on the door. Elena urged me to go down the old back stairs. I had to be careful for they were well warn. I hadn't gone far when I heard Marcus with Elena. He was frantic, told her they had to leave, right away. To grab a change of clothes and be quick about it. I heard Elena shove the bedding out of sight at the top of the stairs, then shut and lock that door. I got you into my car, didn't even bother with seat belts. I kept the car around the side, so no one would have noticed it. I idled down the drive, without lights, and sped up once I was on the road. The only place I could think of to go was to my sister's place. I hadn't gone far when Marcus's car passed me."

Adam saw his mother's face, and the faint tears. She said, "Of course I let you and my sister stay. I never said a word about them when I went out. Grace had sent Marcus a message, we assumed he had received it, but a week went passed and he hadn't been in touch."

"She began to hear rumours," Grace went on. People Marcus dealt with regularly, hadn't heard from him and he wasn't answering his phone. Also that others beside the police were looking for him. Of course people recalled Bennett's behaviour at the dance. He considered Elena his fiancé before he went off and enlisted. But that had been all one sided. It had always been Marcus she wanted. There were lots of other rumours, linking him to some conspiracy, but most of it was just talk."

"So, no one really knew anything," Grant summarised.

"No, but about a month after they vanished, someone ransacked the place I owned," Grace admitted. "I had not lived there since Kim was born. I had been a daily before that. I had a friend living there. It shook me up because I knew it had to be connected to the disappearance, but I don't know who found out I was connected to Marcus. My friend was okay, and I pretended I had just returned from a trip overseas. I cleaned up the mess, understood why my friend wanted to move away, and settled back in here."

Janice took up the narrative again. "We decided it was too

Grace asked, "What happened? What has changed with you?"

"I am not sure. It just seems that once I knew that my dreams were real, the fog in my head seemed to vanish. Now, I need to know the whole truth."

Grace looked to Janice for confirmation, and she took her sister's hand for give moral support.

"Then I guess I should start," Grace said. "Do you remember what I used to be?"

"My nanna," Kim said at once. "You looked after me, most of the time."

"Yes, Marcus and Elena trusted me. Before you came I had been their housekeeper. He had reasons, he never fully explained to me, for keeping is marriage a secret and you when you arrived. I helped deliver you at home, and agreed to stay on in a new role. You were bright little thing, until that night."

"When the couple disappeared?" Grant asked.

Grace stopped talking, seeming to be thinking back in time. "Yes. They had gone to the Harvest Dance, dressed in clothes they had found in trunks. It was the first time they had gone out since you were born. They thought it would be okay, but something happened there and they left early."

"Bennett made a scene," Kim stated.

"How did..."

Grant answered, "I did a bit of research on-line, it was mentioned in an article when people realised the Rymans were missing."

"Well, they came home and told me to pack up some stuff for you, and get you away until he called me. I was to send a message when I found a place. So I was doing that, when I realised you had slipped out. I found you on the stairs, and heard the argument downstairs. That man, Bennett, had followed them home."

"He threw a vase," Kim told her. "I think he must have knocked my father down."

"Yes. I heard the crash. I took you back to the nursery, got you into a coat, and lifted you and the bag I'd packed, intending to go out the side door. I waited a bit until the noise stopped. Marcus had sent Bennett off. Elena came up to tell me the way was clear. That

Chapter 12: Behind the Dreams

They didn't expect to see Janice Laurensen, Adam and Kim's mother, visiting with her sister when they returned. Janice studied Kim as she came in with Paula, then looked away.

Adam asked the question, "Does my step-father know you are here?"

"Of course I told him I was visiting my sister," Janice said calmly. "He is very strong on family responsibility."

Adam scowled.

His aunt spoke quietly. "I asked her to come here, since what I need to say, concerns her too. SO pull up chairs. I take it you are happy to let your friends hear this too."

"Yes," Kim said, asserting herself before Adam could answer. "Why did you never tell me I was adopted?"

"Sit down first and I will try to explain," Grace insisted. Now she was studying Kim, aware of the change in her.

"Why don't you tell me what led to the question?"

Kim seemed to be choosing her words, so Grant began with their decision to hike to Golden Falls, and intimated that finding the house was by chance. Adam mentioned the thunderstorm, so both his mother and aunt would be aware of how it might have affected Kim.

Then Kim was ready. "We saw inside the house. All those things I kept telling you, that you said to forget, or were just dreams. They weren't. The room I kept seeing? It was there! What you called nightmares? Were real. Being there brought even more back."

"But...you were only three," Janice said, staring in disbelief.

"Mrs Laurensen, I've known Kim a long time and I think, in spite of the issues she's had, she must have a very good memory. Ask her something you don't expect her to remember."

"What did I make for your birthday dinner last year?"

"That was six months ago, but Kim said, "Meatloaf with whole eggs inside. I told you it didn't taste like normal and you insisted you used the same recipe as always but you had put eggplant in it. That's what I could taste and why I threw up afterwards."

Janice's jaw dropped open.

"Yes, I think so."

"I think then, that you could have a lot of fun paying back certain people."

Kim considered the idea. "I don't think that is really me. I will keep being quiet, attentive and next time there is an in class test, I can surprise people then. But as far as payback, I will make Haydn an exception. Turn the other cheek with him is getting tiring. "

Grant soon caught up to them, trotting but still carrying his pack easily.

"Do you guys think Bennett knows what happened to the Rymans?" Paula asked. "He said he didn't Kill Elena, so does that mean he knows they are dead?"

"They have been declared dead, we know that. I guess that means everyone now assumes they are. I got my phone to research that dam above the falls, the whole thing was highly contentious. Ryman was dead set against it."

"But it didn't get built until some years later," Adam pointed out. "I think this is more personal and the dam happened by default."

Grant plugged bot earbuds into his ears and asked his phone, "Browneyes, is Marcus Ryman dead or alive."

He kept walking, but the others were eager to hear what came up.

"Now, that's interesting," Grant commented, removing the earbuds, and pocketing them and his phone. "Marcus and Elena were declared officially dead five years after they went missing. That would be eight years ago. If I am not mistaken, construction of the dam began eight years ago."

"It's all conjecture," Adam said. "Is it really relevant this far on? It doesn't help prove whether or not Kim as a Ryman."

"No, but I am not quitting this mystery half way through," Grant promised. "We know something no one else knows. "

"Except Bennett," Paula needled him.

"He had no proof either," Grant pointed out. "That wasn't the point I was going to make. I intend to find proof, for Kim's sake, and Adam. We need to hear what your Aunt Grace has to say."

"I'm sure she has been keeping secrets all this time. " Adam insisted.

"So has Mum," Kim spoke up.

of clarity. It's like I was two people at once."

"So, who are you now," Grant asked, gently.

"I'm still me, Kim. It's just that now I know who I was. Have you rung Aunt Grace yet?'

"No. I will try again." Adam punched her number into his phone.

"Hi Aunt Grace. It's Adam. No, nothing is wrong. I just needed to ask you something and I need the absolute truth...Was Kim adopted? Or is she really my blood sister?"

Adam listened for a while, then asked, "Aunt Grace? Are you still there?"

He listened again. "Fine, we'll be there in ..." he asked Grant the question. "How long will it take to get to town from here?" Adam told his Aunt the estimate and ended the call.

"Well?" Kim demanded.

"She didn't say. All she really said was 'we need to talk'."

"Okay, let's get going," Grant instructed. "The stuff should be a bit dryer, but we will have to dry it more later. I will check inside to make sure everything is turned off, and see the door will lock. We need to get to the road, so we will go down the driveway. Get going. I will catch you up."

Adam did a quick check of the campsite, finished packing what had come out of his pack, but didn't replace the stones from the patio. Grant came out and locked the door, gestured for the others to get going and packed up the rest.

Heading down the driveway, which had never been paved, Paula said to Kim, "I never realised what was going on with you, but I always knew you were more than everyone else saw."

"I know," Kim told her. "I'm glad you never gave up on me."

"It will be interesting to find out how you do at school next week. Can you remember all the history questions? I know you wrote them down."

"I learnt to make that a habit," Kim said. "And, yes. I actually do." She rattled the eight questions off, plus the directions for answering them.

"That is so amazing," Paula said with awe. "What about other things this term?"

"Do I really look that much like Elena Ryman?"

Bennett spun around and stared. "Elena wasn't married."

"I think you might find out she was," Kim insisted.

"No!"

Kim just kept meeting his gaze, the opposite of her normal behaviour towards strangers.

"Your mother...she is still alive?"

"I have no idea. I haven't seen her since I was three. I have always had dreams of my parents, of this house. I dreamt you argued with my parents. Chucked a yellow and blue vase at my father."

Bennett's weathered face turned pale under his tan. "How can you know that?"

"I saw it. I was on the stairs. Something woke me."

Bennet's expression took on a semblance to a cornered animal. He said, hoarsely, "Your parents weren't who you think. I loved your mother, but I didn't kill her."

At that, Bennett turned and stalked from the room. A short while later they heard a car start up.

"What on earth got into you, Kim?" Adam demanded.

"I had to know, and Bennett's reaction is proof. He knew Elena Ryman. I must be very like her."

"And he's one of the suspects to her disappearance." Grant supported Adam.

"Well, he might have argued with them, but they didn't lock him up," Kim said. "Did they?"

"Maybe because no one knew to accuse him of it," Grant pointed out.

"And if he thinks you can prove it, He might not want that fact known," Adam said sharply. "You said he threw a knife at someone. You could be next."

"Not with three witnesses," Kim said with a degree of logic.

"Let's collect our stuff and leave," Paula urged, hoping to stop the staring match between her friend and Adam.

"Adam, that storm last night did more than clear the air," Kim said unexpectedly. "It did something to clear my mind. Until today, I've felt like I was walking through a fog, with only scarce moments

Chapter 11: Secret Exposed

Grant and Paula had seen the photo Kim had found, and were surprised at the likeness of Kim to the woman in the picture. They recalled the talk the previous night, while Kim was asleep, and were all wary of Bennett. All wished Adam had been able to get onto his aunt.

Bennett dished up the bacon and eggs, along with the toast Grant had made using a camp toaster on the kitchen range. Bennett had said there was not much gas left in the tank outside. As he dished, he deigned to admit he needed to wait an hour after his medication before eating.

"I will eat later, but thank you for suggesting I join you. I did have the feeling you planned to leave early."

While the four young adults ate, Bennett kept busy. He switched the BBQ plate for something he could boil a kettle on. When it boiled, he poured some of the boiling water over it to dissolve burnt on fat.

"Where are you all from?" He asked, not looking at them. "Around here?"

"I'm up from the city," Gavin claimed. "Heard about the falls, and decided to visit. I know Adam from Uni. His sister wanted to come and she brought a friend."

"Falls aren't anything now," Bennett grumbled. "Not since the local politicians okayed the dam."

"Is the dam to help farmers?" Paula asked.

"So they say," Bennett confirmed. "Farmers downstream get nothing from it. They don't let out much water from it. They want to keep the water level up in the lake for the rich folk in their condos."

He brought over coffee for grant and Adam and hot chocolate for the girls. He tried not to look at Kim,

Kim didn't immediately take hers, instead, she seemed to study Bennett. "What is it about me that makes you look at me, but not look at me?"

"I don't know what you mean."

"Do you know what happened to them?"

Bennett stopped moving, spatula poised, bacon sizzling. "No. I wish I did."

At a glance from Adam, Grant went to where Bennett was cooking on a camp style mini BBQ.

"Need a hand? I'm told I cook a mean piece of toast."

"If you like," Bennett said, his attention back on his cooking. He flipped the bacon from the pan into a pile keeping warm in a metal saucepan. He added the eggs to another.

Paula edged to the table and sat on a chair next to the wall. Kim took the one opposite. Paula hissed across the table, "What are you doing, silly? If he knows anything the police don't, he won't tell you and if he thinks we know things he's hiding..."

"If he knows something, I want to know it."

"We will," Kim insisted. "We have to if we are to have the life we want. I love you, Adam."

"Kim, it is not that simple. If you were formally adopted, we will still be considered brother and sister. That is all that he will consider."

"Oh!"

"I'm going to ring Aunt Grace."

"Okay," Kim said, slumping.

When the others woke, they all got up and went to view the wreckage of their camp. The fire was well and truly out, both tents had collapsed and were holding a puddle of water. Water had seeped inside, drenching sleeping bags, hiking sleep foam mats, and blankets.

Gavin filled in the toilet hole, taken down the canvas privacy tent and retrieved the guide rope.

"I was hoping to leave before breakfast," Gavin admitted, "But we need to dry to dry our stuff a bit."

"It's not as warm as yesterday, but the sun's out. Can we rig some lines to hang our stuff over? It might dry a bit," Paula suggested.

"Kim, are you okay with us staying here a bit longer?" Adam asked.

Kim had been quiet, but seemed more grounded that morning.

"Yes, let's stay for breakfast. Anything is better than muesli bars."

"OK, we'll pack what we can, and hang the rest in the sun," Adam summed up.

They finally returned inside, to the smell of eggs and bacon cooking, and the kitchen table set for four. Kim followed the others in, noticed the four places and surprised her friends by saying, "Aren't you joining us, Mr Bennett?"

Bennet turned, and looked directly at Kim. "I...you might feel uncomfortable if I did."

"Why would we?" she asked, though it sounded like a challenge.

"Well, you don't really know me," he said as he looked away.

"That's true. Did you once know the people who lived here?"

"I...yes, I knew them."

In spite of the disturbed night, Adam was awake early. His dreams had been highly erotic and totally inappropriate. Still, while the others were still asleep, he lay awake. As much as he tried to tell himself that the way he felt about Kim should be nauseating, all he felt was an irrational hope. But he still couldn't go home and announce, "Hey, Kim isn't my sister." They had grown up together as brother and sister. His step-father believed they were. His mother had never said Kim was anything else. If Kim was Marcus Ryman's daughter, how had she come to live with his mother? He checked his watch. Still too early to ring his aunt to ask the question keeping him sleepless.

He heard rustling, and saw Kim's tousled head emerge from behind the couch. "Sleep well?" he asked quietly.

"Yes, once the storm passed."

"Any dreams?"

"No. But...I understand things now."

"Oh?"

"Remember what I told you since coming here?"

Adam nodded.

"It's often like that. I see things, ordinary things, and suddenly, I am seeing them. The people I mentioned – the smiling man, the beautiful woman. A casual remark turns into their voices in my mind. I hear them speaking to me and I am so happy. Those people I saw by the river, they were Marcus and Elena."

"You can't be sure. You have never seen them."

Kim took the photo she found from under her jumper. "I found this in a room upstairs. They are the people I keep seeing."

Using his small torch, Adam looked at what Kim held. Stared at it. Then Looked at Kim's face. No one could deny the resemblance. Somehow he managed to stop his jaw dropping.

"I'm not mad," Kim told him. "The vivid dreams are memories of a long time ago. I never understood what I was seeing, now I do. I am remembering what I saw and heard. Your mother told me to forget the dreams – they weren't real. Tonight, everything fell back into place. The people I keep seeing are my parents."

"It has to be," Adam said, his voice unsteady. "Yet we still can't prove it."

Chapter 10: Beginning to Understand

"All I recall, is her coming to live with us. I was only about five, I hadn't figured out where babies came from, when I was told she was my sister...I assumed that's how you got a younger sibling."

"That was nearly 14 years ago," Grant considered. "I can't remember much from when I was that old, let alone younger."

"Didn't you say, the couple who lived here were engaged, not married?" Paula challenged Grant. "And had no children?"

"Nothing I read about them mentioned a child," Grant reiterated. "You say the room you saw was a child's room?"

"Yes. Though the bed was stripped down to the mattress, and there was only one toy on a shelf. A small set of drawers had a lot of toys like come with kid's meals."

"Those might have come from an earlier occupant of the room," Paula suggested.

"Not likely. The house belonged to Marcus Ryman and had been in the family for generations. I doubt those sort of toys were around when Marcus was a kid," Grant decided.

They fell silent, concentrating on the new mystery.

"So, if Kim did live here once, and the missing couple were her parents, how can we prove it? Should we even try?" Paula asked.

"If you ask me," Adam said. "I think we do need to. For Kim's sake."

"Proving it will be the thing," Grant said, considering. "First though, you need to ask your mother a question."

"I intend to ask Aunt Grace, first thing in the morning. I don't want my step-father learning I was asking."

"No," Gavin agreed. "If we get the answer we suspect, it will still be hard to prove it. I'd say DNA, but there is no one around to compare it to."

"We can think on that tomorrow. Away from here," Adam told them. Let's try to sleep. I think we need to leave as early as possible." The other two nodded.

Adam collected all the cups and put them in the kitchen. When he returned, the others were all rolled up in blankets and he copied their example.

Grant stood and walked over to one side of the fireplace. "What do you make of this?"

Adam leant forward to look, but needed to go closer.

"It could be where a knife struck the wall," Grant suggested.

Adam stumbled back to the chair.

"Kim's dreams have always been vivid," Adam said. "Today, when she was upstairs, she insisted it wasn't a dream."

"A memory," Paula suggested.

"It has to be," Adam agreed. He told them the things she had often asked him about. "I went upstairs. The room she described... it's here."

"She used to live here," Paula realised. "Is that why she asked about Golden Falls?"

Adam shrugged at that.

Grant asked, "Was she adopted?"

For a long moment, Adam thought back.

from his face. What else had Kim seen? How could Kim have seen the visions she had described? Was she psychic?

He found the partly open door to the bathroom, and made use of the room, then went on to check the rest of the rooms that he hadn't already been in when getting mattresses. The door at the end was partly open, he pushed it the rest of the way and shone his torch around.

"My God!" he breathed, seeing evidence of Kim's dream. No wonder she had freaked.

"That meant..." His heart began to beat frantically. It meant Kim might not be his sister.

With unsteady fingers, he took out his phone and found his Aunt Grace's phone number. He was about to call, but realised the time. First thing in the morning, he promised himself.

Calling his mother wasn't an option. Not if his step-father got to hear the question. When he had married his mother, he had been told Kim was his sister.

In an almost daze, he returned to the living room.

"Kim's asleep," Paula told him quietly.

Adam gestured her to come closer. Grant said, "You look like you've seen a ghost."

"I feel like I have," Adam admitted. "I think I understand what is happening to Kim. And maybe, we shouldn't have come here."

"I'm a bit scared," Paula put in. "Kim has been avoiding Bennett but he's been watching her. Not directly, but sort of out of the corner of his eye."

"It fits. She was telling me not to trust him, and except for what you just said, I didn't sense anything off about him."

"So, what's the mystery?" Grant asked.

"Kim said this place suggested things to her. I think she knows what happened here. I don't know how. But outside, Bennett spooked her. When the storm woke her, she had been having a vivid dream of a man like Bennett, throwing a vase at another man. Though she changed it to a knife. The vase was blue and yellow. I found this on the floor where the couch had been." Adam pulled out the piece of ceramic.

Bennett was out in the kitchen when they had Kim back down in the living room. She was looking all around.

"He's making us a drink," Grant explained, from where he was sprawled in a chair.

To Kim, Adam said, "Go curl up on one of the mattresses. You will soon be warm. We will talk later. Paula, you take the outer mattress, okay?"

"Fine by me," she agreed.

Kim scurried to the mattress by the wall. Paula sat on the couch facing the two chairs on the other side of the fireplace. Adam took the second chair and let out a long breath.

"What's up?" Grant asked quietly.

"Later, okay?" Adam told him.

Since Bennett was returning with the promised drinks, Grant just nodded.

"This will be just what we need," Grant enthused. He sprang up to pass two cups to Paula. Adam feigned a huge yawn as he took his.

"Just put the cups in the sink," Bennett invited. "I can see you all need more rest. I will be upstairs if you need anything."

Adam glanced up and just said, "Thanks." He sipped his drink and stared at the fire, mentally wishing Bennett would hurry up and go upstairs. Then he wondered, what is it about this place?

Kim had said, 'People. Places. Things I don't remember seeing before. I can't have seen before, but yet they are so familiar.' And, a very young Kim had confided, 'Before I sleep I dream of a room with orange curtains and yellow roses on the wall. Animals and toys on a shelf.' He had scoffed then. But now?

He recalled another confidence. 'Did we ever live in a big house with a staircase going up and pictures of men on the wall?' His mind echoed Kim's last words, "And those portraits..."

He put his drink down, grabbed the torch and headed for the stairs. Something had shocked Kim into near catatonia. What else had she seen? He looked down from the stairs, saw the fire and the two matching side tables. He recalled picking up a fragment of blue and yellow porcelain from where the couch had been. He recalled Kim saying, "He threw a vase..."

Adam turned to continue upstairs, but he had felt the blood rush

Chapter 9: The Truth in Dreams

Kim crawled and got to her feet, leaving the bathroom and hurrying to the top of the stairs. Thunder crashed again as she saw Bennett walk into view. He was talking to the boys, but she didn't hear what they were saying. The fire was blazing now, lighting the space below.

The switch in her mind showed her a woman, dressed in an old fashioned style, facing Bennett. She wasn't smiling, Somehow, Kim sensed she was afraid.

"I can't go with you, Gene." She stood her ground until Bennett moved closer.

"I love you, Elena. You are all that kept me going while I was away. You promised to wait for me."

"Marcus," the woman pleaded, desperately.

The man she recognised, stood up, as if he had been on the floor. He moved unsteadily to drag Bennett away from Elena. The men wrestled, Elena moved away. Bennett's voice rose in desperation and threat.

Someone was shaking her. "Kim! Kim!"

Then, "Adam! Come here."

Adam looked up, saw the girls. Kim was like a catatonic statue. He trotted up the stairs, tried to get Kim to respond, finally she stirred.

"I'm scared," she whispered. "I saw it again. My dream. It happened here."

"It was a dream, Kim," Adam insisted.

"No! It happened. It happened here. He...Bennett...was there, with them. With the man and the woman. Why am I seeing it?"

The answer was still eluding her. She was trembling. "And the portraits..." that came out as a whisper.

"Adam? What's wrong?" Paula asked. "It's not just the storm. Is she alright? She has been strange since we got here."

"Later, Paula. I don't know what's wrong, but I need to find out. Let's get back downstairs. We have the mattresses near the fire, and moved the couch to give you girls some privacy. We should all try to sleep some more."

pulled it out further, felt through a mess of childish things. One flash showed her what was in her hand. The cheap toys that come with kids meals at some restaurant chains. She felt further, found what felt like a book. The next flash showed her a kid's diary with its easy to open tiny lock. She felt through some more, hearing the sound of something heavy being moved out of the room next door. Her fingers then felt something flat and slightly flexible, like a card. They tingled and she drew it out.

Paula called to her, and Kim quickly pushed the book down the front of her jeans and the card in her pocket, before emerging from the room.

"Can I have that?" Kim asked, her hand out for the torch.

"Sure. I'll be right going down. Just a heads up though, the water that comes when you flush is brown."

Kim disappeared into the bathroom and locked the door. She took out the card. It was actually a photo pasted onto cardboard. The strength ebbed from her legs. And she sank to the floor.

In the photo was the smiling couple. The same ones who haunted her dreams and the inexplicable visions. With her new realisation that the bedroom of her night visions was real, came the sure knowledge that she was connected to the people in the photo. But how, she asked herself.

For the first time, she realised there was a kind of fog in her mind. She tried to imagine a wind, blowing it away. All she succeeded in doing was recall the etched heart on the tree, 'Marcus loves Elena and K'. Not Anok as the others saw it. It was 'and K'...'and Kim.'

Could her inner conviction be true? She wasn't Adam's sister? That loving him as she craved, wasn't the path to hell and damnation?

"Adam!" she whispered. "Adam..."

Once they were put of sight, he paid attention to Grant quizzing Bennett.

"If the owners of this place just vanished, what happened to all their stuff?"

"I'm told it all got put into storage, though that wasn't until they had been gone almost a year. The place was broken into three or four times before then. Someone must have cleaned out the fridge too, since I didn't find it full off long gone off food. When the estate finally put it on the market, I think they had someone come in and get rid of the worst of the dust."

"They still have paintings on the wall," Adam remarked.

"So I saw. Probably figured no one would want to pinch pictures of stern faced old men. Not sure I want them either."

The fire was starting to take a life of its own, and Bennett got stiffly to his feet.

The girls found the bathroom by opening doors as they went along the passage, though they didn't look in the room Bennett said he was using. Paula went in first, taking the torch.

"I'll wait out here," Kim told her.

With some light coming from below, it wasn't completely dark, though seeing detail wasn't possible. A flash of white light from further along the passage confused her, before she guessed a door was ajar. Something drew her there, to push the door open further. Just as she moved inside, a brighter flash of lightning brought light in through the open curtains.

White walls with yellow flowers, orange curtains, a lone stuffed animal on a wall shelf.

Kim gasped and grabbed the door frame. Something clicked in her mind. It was the room she saw, each night as she was going to sleep. It was real!

 Her feet took her in further, instinctively stopping before her shins hit the side of the small bed, and missing the arm chair next to it.

With the next flash, she saw the cover on the chair, and the mattress stripped of all bedding. Across the room, she saw again the dusty stuffed dog, drooping on the shelf. Between the bed and the chair, a small set of drawers. The top one was part way out. She

Chapter 8: Message from the Past

The lightning continued to flicker, almost continuously. Thunder rumbled.

From outside, they heard, "Are you young people alright? There is plenty of room in the house."

Adam agreed without hesitation. Kim would be better off inside, out of the storm. Grant and Paula emerged, and called out. "Thanks, we'll come in."

Adam and Kim followed. The rain had eased, but they were all soaked by the time they reached the side door of the house. Everyone had their packs, but they had left the sleeping bags.

Bennet handed a torch to each of the boys as they came in the door. Then he led them through a kitchen to an oak panelled living room. The light in there was from the hurricane lamp, set on a table at the far end. It illuminated half the room, including the base of a wooden staircase. The rest of the area was in shadow.

"I'll get the fire going down here," Bennett offered. "It should be okay. I had the chimney checked last week. I have spare mattresses upstairs, if you lads would help me get them down."

"Sure," Adam agreed. "We appreciate the offer. I was beginning to wonder if the second tent would stand up to the rain."

"Well, I really don't mind the company," Bennett said as he added wood from a metal box by the fire place, to the fire he was building. "Feel free to have the run of the house. I'm using the first room at the top of the stairs. There is a bathroom further along. There is one off the kitchen too. They use tank water."

"Now, that's an inviting idea," Paula said, grabbing a torch from Grant.

"Yes, it does. Is there warm water?" Kim asked.

Bennett turned a bit. "Sorry, not at the moment."

"Oh, well. I'll come up with you, Paula."

Adam noticed Kim was keeping on the far side of Paula. She sounded a bit tense, back to her 'in company' normal. He didn't understand why she'd kept saying trust him." He watched the girls go up the stairs, the torch light illuminating the stairs and the lower edges of picture frames.

you should go visit Elena's mother. Though you'd need to tread carefully. I did hear she's been in the care home since a few years after Elena disappeared."

"Thank you, Mr Bennett," Kim told him. "I know this has dredged up said memories."

"And yet, seeing you, so like her. It's like the sun can shine again. I never knew about you. I don't think anyone ever did."

"We'll keep in touch," Kim promised.

"Bray," Grant said thoughtfully, as he drove his car back to Twin Falls. "Bennett may not think he could be corrupt, but if you think on it, and if he is and people found out, he's got a heck of a lot to lose."

"And we had better not try to face him without knowing a lot more about him," Adam warned, intending the comment at Kim.

"I'll have a word with my mate, Murph," Grant promised.

"We can't do much more this weekend," Adam voiced. "Unless we sit down and decide what information we need. We might now know Kim's parentage, have a birth certificate and a photo that shows her like she is to Elena, but that's not enough to prove she really is the child of Marcus and Elena."

"There's Mum and Aunt Grace," Kim said.

"I know, but I don't want them to get put in the middle of this," Adam told her.

That gave Kim a sense of dread. "Maybe we should get them to make some kind of formal declaration to keep safe."

"Actually, it's a really good idea," Grant agreed. "I took photos at the house and those notes. I wonder if we can get hold of police records."

"One way we can prove if Kim is Elena's daughter," Paula spoke up. "DNA."

"Without her parents being found?" Adam pointed out.

"If Elena's mother is still alive, that should be a good indicator."

"There's still a problem," Adam persisted. "We can't march up to a total stranger, which is really what she is, and ask for a DNA sample. Maybe we could talk to the nursing staff, but someone might get to hear of it."

"I think we really need to work something out to do that," Kim said. "If I am her granddaughter, she deserves to know about me."

"I have to agree," Adam told her. "Let's give that problem some thought."

They continued to brainstorm ideas with each providing ideas until they ran out of things to say. When they were nearly home, Kim said, "Something is confusing me."

"What's that?" Adam prompted.

"That night when Marcus and Elena went off," she began. "Bennett came and broke the vase. I don't think he have thrown the knife. If he had one, and he was angry, he'd have thrown that."

"So who threw the knife?" Paula blurted.

"Maybe that didn't happen then, but if someone came after Bennett left, and did that, I'm not surprised they fled when they could."

"Exactly," Kim said. "Except, they didn't leave all that long after Aunt Grace. So obviously, they overcame the assailant. Assuming that, did Marcus stop to take personal papers?"

"I'd guess he didn't. He may not have had anything kept there," Grant considered.

"So, if the assailant wasn't dead, and came wanting something thought to be there, why didn't they search the place then?" Kim asked. "Bennett, when he came back, didn't see signs of that."

They all proposed possible scenarios until Grant said, "Let's take a step back. Kim heard hammering on the door. That suggests urgency..."

"Or someone trying to terrorise," Paula broke in.

"Fine. Let's just assume someone heard of a threat to them, hurried over with a warning, and someone came in stealthily and threatened them all. The knife got thrown. The attack was overcome, then they went off. The attacker woke up, expected police and took off. Then went back later."

"That is good as our other scenarios," Adam told him. "Though Marcus might have been aware of danger, but may not have lined up a bolt hole. If a friend did come to warn him, he might have told them a place to go."

"And betrayed them," Kim finished. "Do you think that was Bray? That Bray was the one leaking stuff to others."

"It might be," Paula said. "Check later, but the last comment in the journal mentioned Bray."

"But if they didn't trust him, why go where he said," Kim put in.

"We don't know if they did," Grant pointed out. "But maybe Bray went with them to show them the way. And Marcus didn't know Bray was betraying him, just had a suspicion. If Bray was a long-time friend, seemingly risking his neck to warn Marcus, the hurry, hurry pressure probably didn't let Marcus think things through."

"Well, that's all the more reason to have information about him before we go near him," Adam reiterated.

Chapter 18: The New Kim

Grant spoke to his friend, Murph, who agreed to help for no cost. They arranged to meet to pass on any results, using a USB not by phone or computer. Some information came immediately, and it indicated there had been corruption happening a decade back, especially related to the building of the dam and the creation of the lake. He didn't give details, since the names he'd heard whispered didn't include Bray.

The week at school seemed endless to Kim. Her new knowledge and the myriad of questions it spawned had distracted, so few noticed how she had changed. A few of the teachers did, but made no comment. One teacher had a particularly rowdy class, where several dominant boys where claiming she had not said work had to be in that day. She'd queried the girl next to Kim, but Tansy was just too scared of the boys to refute their claim. Kim put a hand up and received permission to speak. She stood and recited what the teacher had said, word for word. The boys just gaped.

At break, they sauntered up and jostled her, calling her 'retard' as they often did.

A teacher coming nearer caused them to step back. And Kim had calmly said, "If you three don't go away and stop bullying me, I will tell the principal who it is bullying the year sevens."

"You wouldn't dare," the largest of the three jeered.

"And if you continue to harass them, I'll even mention how you cheated on the last two maths exams."

"Is there a problem here?" the teacher asked mildly. The boys said a hasty 'no' and ran off.

"Kim?" the teacher asked kindly.

"No problem at the moment," Kim told her, looking directly at the teacher. Something her former self never did.

By the end of the day, those boys had created trouble for her. Kim had never been in trouble and most people considered her 'special needs'. Therefore the PA announcement during afternoon homeroom for her to attend the front office, surprised everyone. The three bullying boys snickered and jabbed each other.

Paula was not unaware of the boy's behaviour, but her frie hadn't mentioned trouble that day.

"I'm with you," she told Kim.

Kim collected her bag and immediately trotted to the office. She saw Adam lounging nearby, concern evident in his expression. He just stared when Kim winked him.

Facing the stern but kindly expression of the principal, gave her no qualms. He was nice compared to her stepfather. She guessed he was being kind to the 'special needs' girl, by how he phrased his reprimands.

First he explained, he'd received complaints about her, and spoken to a number of younger students who claimed she was the one who extorted money from them and a list of other petty bullying tactics.

Then he expressed his disappointment, told her that her behaviour was unacceptable and a continuation of it would have consequences.

Paula who insisted on being present, and he'd promised not to interrupt, could not keep quiet any longer. New Lauren "Kim would never do any of that!"

"Miss Paula, let Miss Laurensen speak for herself," came the reprimand, followed by a request directed at Kim. "What do you have to say for yourself?"

"Sir, Henry, James and Brad started trying to belittle me in year 7, and continue to do so. Today I spoke to them, told them if they didn't leave me alone, I tell you how they bully the youngest students. Mrs Trent came by then so they ran off. If they told you I was bullying younger kids, it is to get me in trouble. They could easily frighten some into saying it was me."

During this, Kim had kept her head down, like people were used to seeing her.

Kim's form teacher had noticed the change in Kim during class, but this speech was the longest she had heard from her. She kept quiet. The principal was astounded too, but he seemed unsure how to react. He had not expected what he heard.

"If the boys have been bullying you, why have you never said anything?"

"Sir," Kim raised her head to look at straight at him, which he found it particularly disconcerting. "I was taught at home to turn the other cheek. I let them have their fun, and frankly, I usually forgot it soon anyway."

Paula knew that was a lie, but said nothing then.

"Names didn't bother me, but I saw them annoying some year sevens this morning and realised no one else would stand up to them. So I did!"

Her stance was belligerent, but Paula and Kim's class teacher wanted to cheer.

"Do you realise, young lady, that threatening other students is also bullying?"

Kim wants to laugh at him. "I finally do what people advise, stand up to those bullies and you tell me I'm the bully now? Well, maybe they took as a threat. What it was, was a piece of advice, a chance to realise the error of their ways, and stop bullying younger kids."

The direct look Kim gave the principal definitely made him uncomfortable.

"I will be having a talk with your parents, Miss Laurensen," he told her. "I'm concerned that you are not taking your medication."

"I'm not on medication," Kim told him, but her words seemed to convince him of something.

"I will insist on having your parents take you to see your specialist. I will have a letter for you to take home."

Kim turned and walked out current ignoring the demand she returned. Adam went after her, attempting to calm her down. He hadn't seen her like this either. In tears yes, often. He now realised that was frustration.

"Kim, Mrs Hickory wants to talk to you."

She stopped striding away but didn't turn to face her teacher.

"Kim?"

"What is it?"

"There were a lot of complaints."

"They are all lies!" Kim tried not to yell and to keep her tears in check.

"You have been different this week."

"So, are you saying because I'm different, I've also become a bully?"

"No, I'm not suggesting that. I am wondering what has happened to you."

Kim let her anger ebb.

"I feel different. Until the last few days, my mind has seemed to be full of fog. Now it's clearer. Not perfectly, but enough that I can understand things better. And it's not because I stopped medication, or changed it or saw a psychiatrist, who obviously hasn't been doing any good."

"What do you think it was?" Mrs Hickory was anxious to know.

Kim didn't want to mention the weekend in case details got back to her father. "I went to visit my aunt in Twin Falls, and there was a terrible thunderstorm. The mind fog seem to start breaking up."

"Perhaps the school psychologist would be a better person to see," Mrs Hickory suggested. "She's worked with you, and can run tests again and compare results."

"Maybe you can tell the principal that," Kim suggested in return. "I can't believe he believed bullies over someone they pushed around for years."

Mrs Hickory let the disrespectful comment pass. The girl had a point. The boys she named had been the ones to make the initial complaint. They were amongst the top students academically, came from well off families, and obviously were smart enough to hide what they did.

The storm that erupted when they got home was a 100 times worse. Adam figured the principal had rung his stepfather for as soon as Kim returned and put her school bag in stand, he ordered her into his office. Loitering in the hall, Adam could hear the raised voices and wondered if his step-father would control the impulse to hit out.

When Kim came out, red faced, and raced upstairs, he couldn't tell. He followed her up, knocked on her door, and got told to 'go away!'. He decided to leave her alone to calm down.

But when he went for her room a short time later and heard the convulsive sobs, well into the hiccupping state, his own resolve hardened. He went downstairs and knocked on the closed door of his father's office.

Adam pushed away the memory of his last time in there, refused to consider he might earn a repeat and forged ahead.

"Will you let me go and calm Kim down? She's crying so hard she's hiccupping and beyond being able to stop."

"No!"

"With all due respect, Sir. I can calm her and it's not by doing anything you think I'm likely to stoop to."

"Her mother can talk sense to her."

"Mum is not here? And I don't think Kim will listen to her right now."

"It is time your sister grew up and takes responsibility for her actions. It seems she is not as backward as she's had us believe."

Adam clamped his mouth shut until he thought he would manage to speak civilly.

"The principal rang you didn't he?" Adam accused.

"That is no business of yours."

"With respect, yes it is. As you've reminded me quite often recently, she's my sister. I'm her elder and should look after her. Whatever the principal told you, I don't believe is a true summary of events."

"Principal Montgomery is an Elder of the church. Are you accusing him of lying? Of bearing false witness?"

"I am saying he's misunderstanding what actually happened," Adam phrased his reply. "Paula was with her when Principal Montgomery was talking to her and she told me that Kim told him the absolute truth, and he didn't believe her."

"I don't accept being rude to teachers and the school principal as proper behaviour. Do you?"

"No, not normally. In this instance, he was wrong. Kim has never been in trouble at school. Surely that should have given her the right to be listened to."

"And I have noticed a change in her since we spoke on Friday last. I do not like it."

"I've noticed that same change and I think it was a blessing," Adam's saw his step father about to speak. "Please hear me out. Kim told me, when I mentioned it that until this weekend her mind seemed foggy. So that's why she used to forget things. I don't know if it is because she and Paula their own way to Twin Falls and back has given her a new confidence in herself, or if it's from something else. What is good is that she chose today to stand up for herself, rather than let certain bullying classmates treat her like dirt. What is also good is she's comprehending classes with greater ease. I heard from Paul that she'd spoken up for one of her teachers, Mrs Morrison, when a certain three boys were disrespecting her. She repeated word for word what the teacher told the class about an assignments due date. I found that particularly surprising. I don't think treating that blessing as a further mental aberration, is right. Did you ever let Kim tell you her reasons for today?"

"You're being insolent!" Jeremiah Laurensen said.

"No, Sir, I was asking a question."

Adam could tell that his step-father's initial anger had cooled and breathed easier.

Chapter 19: Kim Faces her Step-father

"Go and help your sister. I'll talk with her again later."

"Thank you."

Adam breathed a deep breath and went to fetch a bottle of water. He got no response at first with his polite knock, so he calls through the door, "Let me in before you give yourself a heart attack. It's okay, I have permission."

He heard the sobs and hiccups getting louder and the door being unlocked. Kim threw herself at him, then tried to kick the door shut.

Adam allowed himself to accept the hug, for longer than he should, before saying, "Sip some water, and sit down before you black out."

"I don't want the door open!" Kim managed to say between sobs.

"I was allowed to come and help you," he said in a normal voice, then lowered it. "I don't guarantee he won't come to check. With the door open, he can't cast a dispersions, okay?"

Kim nodded and concentrated on calming down. Already had a foul headache.

"He says he will speak to you again."

"He can go to hell," Kim said under the her breath.

"I think he will listen to your side of the story this time. Keep it respectful, okay? And if you can now record every bit of Christian behaviour we've been taught, refer to it."

"Feed him his own sermons?" Kim suggested.

"I think he needs to hear it," Adam said seriously, but with an inner malicious intent.

The lingering resentment Adam felt towards his stepfather from the previous week, vanished. He could hardly believe his ears when his step-father actually apologised to Kim. His sister seemed to have reverted to her former usual self, keeping her eyes down, not looking at anyone. Hearing the apology, had her abruptly looking at the speaker, regardless of the still red-rimmed eyes.

It was actually even more astonishing that he spoke in front of the rest of the family.

"After considering my earlier comments you, Kim, I realised I was spurning a blessing from our Lord by not listening to you."

While Jeremiah had glanced at Adam in approval, not approbation, his focus was on Kim.

"Please tell me about your day at school."

Kim glanced at Adam, saw his nod, and began speaking quietly. Their step-father merely listened without interrupting. Adam watched his face, particularly when Kim mentioned reasons which were, as he suggested, throwing his sermons back in his face. Yet, with each such occasion, his expression seemed to change. Maybe he was realising that this step-daughter, really had taken in the Christian doctrines.

It wasn't really a lie, Adam told himself. Kim was a sweet person who, until now, was frustrated by things beyond her control.

Now, too, their step-father was coming to realise her unusual memory, for she gave him details of things the three boys in her class threatened young kids with to get their way.

Kim impressed him further by answering his questions with brutal honesty. Her recitation of the torments she had endured from Henry, Brad and James, sparked the first signs of anger.

"What are the last names of these boys?"

Kim told him.

"I will have Linus Montgomery talk to these boys."

"I felt he believed them," Kim said quietly. "And apart from my word, against that of the popular, intelligent, well-off boys, I cannot provide proof, unless other victims are willing to talk. And those that were terrorised into lying find courage to admit it."

Adam said, "They only pick on people when they know no teachers are around."

"That too is a consideration and typical of those who prey on the weak and disrespect women."

"Aha!" Adam thought. "That's what did it." He kept that thought to consider the later, and said instead, "I know the school has CCTV security about the place. Maybe one or other cameras has picked up something."

It was a risky thing to mention, for while his stepfather accepted electronic devices as a necessary evil, he was a firm believer in privacy.

"Yes. Such as devices should ensure the security of those who attend the school. You may leave this matter with me."

Kim, without the usual politeness, stood up from her position at the table and ran around it to give her step-father a hug. That it made Jeremiah Laurensen look extremely uncomfortable, for he'd never been a demonstrative person, he accepted it. Patting her back until suggesting she might like to have dessert. On her way back, when only Adam would see, she winked.

"Manipulative little thing" he began the thought. Then he smiled inwardly. His mother was right. He was a good man, even if set in his beliefs. He and Kim had just learned how to reach him, without confrontation.

He shivered though. If he ever learnt the full details of the previous weekend, this fragile new truce might not just fail, but shatter.

As the second week progressed as a snail's pace, Adam's impatience to hear from Grant's friend, Murph, intensified.

It was at times like this that he wished his birthday had been a couple of months earlier. Grant had already graduated to university, while he was still sweating and studying for his year 12 exams. At least, Adam told himself, I will have less concerns about Kim when she is at school on her own next year.

While the school was alive with rumours, all most knew was that three of the most popular guys were on suspension. The parents of those boys had been in to talk to Montgomery, and Adam had recognised one set from the odd occasions he decided to attend a Sunday service with his stepdad. Adam didn't know James's situation at home, but Jeremiah Laurensen hadn't insisted that his new wife and her children became part of his church. If James's is parents were both members of the church, he decided he didn't want to be in James's shoes just then.

While waiting for Kim and Paula after school, his phone rang.

"Hi, Grant," was all he said before listening, then, "Sunday. Okay."

When the girls arrived, he said, "Grant will meet us after the Sunday service."

"I didn't know you went," Paula said, uncertainly.

"We did last week, to reward him for being human," Kim told her. "And if Grant meets us there, it won't seem odd us chatting while waiting for step-dad to finish talking to his friends."

"You'd better ring me first thing you get home. You won't get me going to that church."

"I'll get Grant to call you," Adam told her. "I can't wait to see what his friend found out."

Grant hadn't said much when he palmed the USB to Adam when they shook hands. Only murmured, "I reckon Bray is up to his neck in the business. Read that, I've included notes I took when Murph reported. If I were you, I would make an extra copy, and hide it."

Kim had said, "I want to copy too, but I'll rename files like it's stuff for school work."

"I like how you think, new Kim," Grant teased, but with a huge grin.

"But seriously, Murph thinks someone has been watching him for the past few days."

"What about when he gave you the USB?" Kim asked.

Grant tapped his head. "We never met. He dropped it, I picked it up. It was safe the whole time and a gap between both phases."

"Stop talking like a politician," Adam told him.

A glance around suggested he was being careful. He spoke then as if being secretive. "A little bird told me of the fate of three popular ratbags."

"Who told you?" Kim asked.

"A friend of a friend." Grant persisted in being cryptic. In a low voice he added, "James's brother hasn't been his usual arrogant, priggish self this week. His father is a close crony of Bray's." Grant tapped his nose.

It didn't; take Adam or Kim very long to realise a potential source of trouble, if they didn't play their cards right."

Grant saw Jeremiah Laurensen approaching and began heading off, calling back, "You right for the game Saturday?"

Adam told him, "I'll try to be," a moment before his step-father said, "Let us head home to your mother."

Chapter 20: Knowledge from the Journal

Adam's eyes glanced from copied pages of Marcus's journal, to Grant's notes.

"Numbers on this page seem to represent bank accounts. However, likely they have been closed. Two confirmed so."

Adam scrolled on. "These are likely investment related. They appear still active through an investment broking company. "

Other groups of cryptic numbers were still without clues. Then, "These numbers and dollar amounts were opened about when earlier accounts were closed."

It was becoming apparent that Marcus Ryman was indeed suspicious of someone potentially hacking his accounts. A separate section of the notes had, "The investment brokerage has an excellent trust rating. It operates a number of subsidiary companies. Top personnel in all have high trust ratings."

"Huh!" Adam thought, "Sounds too good to be true. I wonder if Murph can dig deeper .I know you can't trust everything online." He kept reading.

In her separate room, Kim went through the copy Adam had made for her. She'd done as she said, renamed the files using a system she devised. Now all the files seemed to be headed by subject, with subtitles for apparently different subjects. She then began going through files, though the explanations of number groups she scan read and moved on. For some reason, a group of numbers with not even a cryptic initial, caught her attention. Mostly because the first four numbers was the year of the date on her birth certificate she now had for Kathryn Ryman. A quick check of the document she'd hidden in her room, proved her theory. They were identical. She scribbled down the other three numbers there, wondering if they were also birth, death or marriage record numbers. Hearing footsteps coming upstairs, she hid the note and switched her computer to her history assignments and opened her history notes.

The knock on the open door, made her turn. Seeing her step-father, gave her a guilty twinge.

"I wanted to see how your school work is going."

"I'm finding it easier," Kim told him. "I still write down lots of notes in class, but I don't have to re-read them a dozen times to remember what I need to answer a question."

"Two of your teachers have told me you are doing so much better. The psychologist is amazed at the improvement. She feels you may not need the same level of help now."

That help had been constant for the past two years, and her first thought was one of panic. Yet the new her, realised she probably didn't need as much help now.

"Maybe I don't," she said, thoughtfully. "Though don't they have funding for Miss Marsden until the end of the year?"

"Yes, that's what I understand. However, I was asked my opinion, and in turn, I am asking for yours."

Kim would have gaped, but the consideration had her speechless for a moment.

"It seems there are several students who might benefit from extra help, if Mrs Marsden had time for extra students."

It was a change she hadn't anticipated and suddenly, the thought of not having Mrs Marsden around was like being thrust adrift in a small boat.

"I...I'm not sure. I want to be like everyone else. I feel more like them now, but sometimes that fogginess seems to be coming back. And next year, I will be in year 12."

"Maybe I suggest fewer sessions until the end of the year, to give you a chance to prove yourself. Then we can talk again next year."

Grant sent Adam and Kim a one word message. "Bingo."

It told them that Kim had been right about the numbers referring to birth, death or marriage registrations. In a call that followed, Grant told Adam he was sending a link to a private site that had the actual information, but it would only be up for 24 hours.

"Is he getting paranoid?" Kim asked.

"More likely just being careful," Adam gave his opinion. "I'll forward the link to you. Then once you use it, delete the message."

"Yes, Sir," Kim jested, meeting his eyes for a moment longer than necessary.

Adam felt a flush rising, but Kim quickly changed the subject. "When is your first exam?"

Adam told her, then told her the date of the last one.

"Well, you had better get back to studying. I have some on-line research to do."

They both knew what she intended and Adam knew he really needed to be studying for his English exam.

Having dates for her real parents births and marriage allowed Kim to look for references in the family notices section of the newspapers. The births were announced in the main dailies, and gave her the names of her grandparents, and the place where both parents were born. The marriage details gave the place of the wedding as the Melbourne registry office. She had searched for articles relating to the Ryman family before, but repeated the searches again using Marcus's father's name. This time she found information relating to his marriage to Marcus's mother, articles about a wild bachelor party and photos from the church and reception. She copied the articles and read each one carefully to get the details in her memory.

One name jumped out at her, Duncan Bray was named as the best man at the wedding of Marcus Ryman senior. It also mentioned he was an up and coming financial wizard. That meant, his son, Marcus probably knew Duncan Bray from a young age and being a friend of his father's probably led to trusting him completely. Estimating Bray's age, put him in his sixties.

Kim sat back as ideas fell into place, all but one. Would Bray have thrown the knife? No, she decided. He would want to keep Marcus ignorant if he could.

She switched her search to Bray, looked up his birth registration and checked for a marriage registration. Like Elena, he came from Twin Falls. Was that significant?

Reaching dead ends, she rang Grant and mentioned a chat online. He came on at once. Kim typed a few words to summarise what she found. He said to erase the message and wait. She did.

Shortly a reply came back. "B gave E away. Rel to Ks"

Kim echoed, "Bingo."